CONSTABLE VERSUS GREENGRASS

A perfect feel-good read from one of Britain's best-loved authors

NICHOLAS RHEA

Constable Nick Mystery Book 16

Revised edition 2021
Joffe Books, London
www.joffebooks.com

First published in Great Britain in 1995

© Nicholas Rhea 1995, 2021

This book is a work of fiction. Names, characters, businesses, organisations, places and events are either the product of the author's imagination or are used fictitiously. Any resemblance to actual persons, living or dead, events or locales is entirely coincidental. The spelling used is British English except where fidelity to the author's rendering of accent or dialect supersedes this. The right of Nicholas Rhea to be identified as author of this work has been asserted in accordance with the Copyright, Designs and Patents Act 1988.

Join our mailing list and become one of thousands of readers enjoying free Kindle crime thriller, detective, mystery, and romance books and new releases. Receive your first bargain book this month!

www.joffebooks.com/contact

We love to hear from our readers! Please email any feedback you have to: feedback@joffebooks.com

ISBN: 978-1-78931-661-2

*Dedicated to Bill Maynard for making Claude
Jeremiah Greengrass such a lovable rogue in Heartbeat.*

1. GREENGRASS ROOTS

. . . the roots of sin are there.
RUDYARD KIPLING, 1865–1936

Researching the history of the Greengrass family of Aidensfield, a picturesque village on the edge of the North York Moors, has provided a fascinating glimpse into the history of that infamous dynasty.

The first recorded Greengrass probably appears in the Bronze Age. Knowledge of this bygone ancestor of Claude Jeremiah Greengrass came in 1846 with the discovery of a man's skeleton during archaeological excavations of a burial mound. It was on Pike Hill Moss, above Aidensfield, and the skeleton of an unidentified breed of dog lay beside the man. Closer examination revealed strands of faded green grass complete with roots and panicles; these were in an earthenware vessel beside the man's body. Initially, it was thought that the man had been a gardener and that the container was a primitive plant pot in which he was trying to cultivate grass, but closer examination revealed the vessel was in the shape of a very large version of a modern pint-sized beer glass with a handle.

The grass, of the variety *Setaria viridis* (green panic-grass) had clearly been fresh when placed in the burial chamber centuries earlier and its root may have enabled it to survive for some time. The grass was of little academic interest. In that era, deceased persons were buried beside the things they treasured; the huge drinking vessel is thought to have been important in the social life of the deceased. The significance of the green panic-grass has continued to puzzle historians.

The drinking vessel, handmade in local clay, might have been the forerunner of the jeroboam, a very large wine container; it bore some crude letter-type markings which appeared to be the name of the owner, *Clod*, and so, also bearing in mind the grass relics, the skeleton was nicknamed Clod Jeroboam Green Grass. Oddly enough, the word "clod" continues to be used to describe a clump of grass which is attached to a lump of earth; it is also used to describe a stupid person, i.e. a clodhopper.

The dog had the skeleton of a brown hare in its mouth along with some remnants of a plant called lucerne or alfalfa, this being a type of fodder. Subsequent examination showed that both man and dog had met a violent death, each having suffered a severe blow to the skull, probably administered by a heavy wooden club. It is thought the pair had been caught in the v of poaching and summarily dealt with. Because of the alfalfa found in its mouth, the dog was called Alf, later expanded to Alfred.

I could not find any further references to Greengrasses until Roman times. The Roman invasion of Britain began around AD 78, and the area around Aidensfield was quickly colonised, with York (Eboracum) and Malton (Derventio) being local centres of great military importance. A military road was constructed across the moors from Appleton le Street near Malton towards the coast at Whitby; the four Cawthorn Camps near Wrelton were built as a base for the soldiers and part of the road they built almost 2,000 years ago can still be seen on Wheeldale Moor above Goathland.

Over a mile and a quarter long, its legendary name is Wade's Causeway, one story being that it was constructed by the giant Wade. In fact, it is one of the finest examples of a

Roman road in this country. It passes very close to Aidensfield and records reveal that an ancestor of Claude Jeremiah Greengrass helped in the construction of this renowned highway. There is no record of a Wade Greengrass, but it is known there existed a man called Claudius Januarius Herbeus, the illegitimate son of a Roman soldier called Pontius Pilate Herbeus and an English girl called Clodasmunda.

She is thought to have been a descendant of the aforementioned Clod who had lived during the Bronze Age. Claudius was named after the renowned Emperor Claudius while Herbeus is the Latin for grass-green, a beautiful shade of that colour. The English version is Greengrass. Thus, with some certainty, the legendary Greengrass dynasty can be dated to Roman times, albeit with the likelihood of some Bronze Age Greengrasses.

Claudius Januarius Herbeus, alias Grassgreen, secured work on the Roman road near what is now called Aidensfield. His first duty was to clear the scrubland so that the road-builders and engineers could proceed without interruption. He was quickly promoted to carrier, his job being to cart stones to the construction site. He had to provide his own horse and flat-bottomed chariot. Always accompanied by his dog, a woolly grey *caninus* called Alfresco, it wasn't long before Claudius was stealing some of the stones and selling them in the nearest village. He was caught, flogged, and ordered to do bathhouse and latrine fatigues.

He was then forced to work longer hours and to fetch more stones. He had to do the work of two men while his dog was forced to haul a small dog cart, also loaded with stones; this prevented it chasing the camp commandant's game and poultry.

Contemporary records of the audited accounts for the road building show the best materials continued to disappear, and that some local English mansions appeared to be constructed from high-quality stones of a type very similar to that obtained especially for this magnificent road. One of the Roman soldiers, a regimental commander called Oscarius

Blaketonicus, carried out a searching investigation but could not secure proof that Claudius Januarius Herbeus, alias Grassgreen, was responsible for removing them.

After the Roman era, the dynasty changed its name from Grassgreen to Greengrass and there are Anglo-Saxon records of a Claude Ethelred-The-Always-Ready Greengrass. An itinerant image-maker, he sold carved gods to the heathens and transferred his skills to making statues when Christianity came to this country. His depiction of his patron saint, St Jeremiah the Cunning, has survived and can be seen in the Ashfordly Museum of Antiquities.

A statue of this Greengrass, carved by himself in stone, was discovered cemented into the walls of an old church c.1346 with a dog asleep at his feet. Apparently hidden in the ninth century for reasons which are unclear, it was also placed in Ashfordly Museum.

It is thought this Greengrass had a son, Claude Sweyne Forkebearde Greengrass but no trace remains; a hint in an old manuscript suggests a man of this name earned a living selling rams' horns to adorn the helmets of the Vikings.

After the Norman invasion of 1066, documents relating to an old church at Aidienesfeld (Aidensfield) show that the man who supplied the stone from which the church was built was a Claude Rufus Greengrass, described as a villain or feudal serf who occasionally worked for the lord of the manor. Without authority, he had removed stones from the Roman road, now disused, and had sold them to the church. Because no owner of the stones could be traced, no prosecution followed. Notes made by a constable of the time indicated that Claude said in court, "I reckon these belong to Julius Caesar and he hasn't complained." It was claimed that the ghost of a Roman soldier, with a stone hanging around his neck on a rope, haunted the church for centuries thereafter. One theory is that it was the ghost of the regimental commander, Oscarius Blaketonicus.

This same Claude, who had a dog called Hardigrasse, is believed to be the felon who was once arraigned before the court of the Manor of Aidienesfeld (Aidensfield) and Eschewathelby (Ashfordly) for an offence, which when translated means "surreptitiously, without permission and by divers unlawful methods, trapping conies in ye coneyries and warrens which are ye property of Robert, Lord of ye Manor of Eschewathelby, and through devilish antics of a dogge Hardigrasse, taking away said conies for sundry mischievous purposes". He was fined fifty shillings, a large sum at that time.

In 1309, a Claude Plantagenet Greengrass was found guilty by the manorial court of refusing to work at the harvest and, along with his dog, Alfalfa, was placed in the stocks. At that time, a man had to mow for one day, hoe for one day, turn hay for one day and in the autumn, reap for three days for a fee of one penny per day. Greengrass had refused, saying the pay wasn't good enough. When in the stocks, the Greengrass dog, Alfalfa, survived by eating rotten chickens hurled at Greengrass. This was considered apt punishment because one of Greengrass's business ventures had been the selling of rotten eggs, vegetables, fish and meat to the crowds which assembled around the village stocks — they threw them at the prisoners. Now Greengrass was getting back some of his own ordure.

Then, in the late 1430s, a Claude Montefiore Greengrass was engaged in the manufacture of jewellery from jet found both on the moors above Aidensfield and on the coast while another, Claude Marco Polo Greengrass, a one-time explorer, earned his living as a fisherman at Whitby; both were sentenced to two days in the pillory for offences which have never been disclosed. It is thought that the jet was not true jet and the fish had been poached from Lord Eschfordeli's stocks. Shortly afterward, the name Ashfordly appeared.

In one of the rare references to a female Greengrass, there is a note in the records of the Elsinby Court Leet for 1622 of a Claudia Jacintha Greengrass being convicted of being a scold, i.e. that she was guilty of lewd behaviour in that she daily caused strife and discord among her neighbours.

The punishment was "that she be soundly ducked on the ducking stool three times over the head and ears by the constables for such misdemeanour". She continued to scold and curse even as she was being lowered into a deep pool in Aidensfield Beck. The water frothed and bubbled on the surface due to her powerful underwater ranting and, because of her violent kicking, the ducking stool had to be repaired. It is said that no fish has since survived in that pool. The stool was repaired by the local carpenter who was her son, Claude Hurstmonceux Greengrass. He specialised in the manufacture and repair of ducking stools, cucking stools, foot stools and milking stools.

One Greengrass who made legal history in the seventeenth century is Half-Hanged Greengrass. His real name was Claude Charlemagne Greengrass and he had been convicted of stealing a sheep which belonged to Lord Ashfordly. Sentenced to be hanged on the gallows on Ashfordly Hill, he recovered while his body was being cut down several hours later, and so the court ordered a retrial. He was found guilty once more and sentenced to be hanged again; for the second time, the gallows were used on Ashfordly Hill and a huge crowd gathered to see the now legendary Half-Hanged Greengrass. On this occasion, the rope snapped and Greengrass fell to the ground where he leapt up and shouted "Greengrass forever! Long live Greengrass!" The crowd loved this demonstration of invincibility. Not to be defeated by Greengrass, however, the authorities swiftly organised a new rope and for the third time, Greengrass was suspended by the neck from Ashfordly Gallows.

On this occasion, he made terrible choking noises and everyone was satisfied that justice had been done. Several hours later, though, as his body lay in the mortuary awaiting disposal on the community midden, he recovered yet again and staggered into the street shouting, "It's a miracle, it's a miracle. Somebody up there loves me!"

Upon hearing the news, Lord Ashfordly regarded these remarkable recoveries as a sign from heaven and ordered the release of Greengrass "on condition he went to live in Buckinghamshire". It is not known whether that branch of the dynasty thrived in their new surroundings although it was recorded that ten sheep, sixteen hens, a horse and a cart all disappeared from Ashfordly Hall at the time of the Greengrass departure to the south.

The name of Greengrass appears in a list of 100 convicts who were transported to New South Wales, Australia, from Chatham in July 1829. He was Napoleon Bonaparte Greengrass who was convicted of stealing a pair of shoes, a side of ham and a sack of potatoes from the outbuildings of Ashfordly Hall, the property of Lord Ashfordly. The parish constable who arrested this Greengrass was called Oscar Blaketon, an ancestor of the Sergeant Blaketon of Ashfordly Police, who is reputed to have said at the trial, "These Greengrasses never learn, Your Worships. There's bad blood in them, mark my words."

Since the formation of the county police force in 1856, court records have been more meticulously maintained and the name of Greengrass appeared many times between 1856 and my time at Aidensfield in the 1960s.

Without going into unnecessary detail, the following are some of the offences:

1859 — Eli Humphrey Greengrass — hawking without a licence. Fined 10s.0d.

1864 — Whittaker Freeman Greengrass — drunk in charge of a horse. Fined 5s.0d.

1869 — Thundercliffe Jasper Greengrass — refusing to quit licensed premises. Fined 5s.0d.

1876 — Osbourne Charles Greengrass — travelling on a train without a ticket. Fined 5s.0d.

1877 — Osbourne Charles Greengrass — fraudulent travel on a tram. Fined 10s.0d.

1890 — Alfred Tennyson Greengrass — shoeing a horse in the street. Fined 3s.6d.

1891 — Alfred Tennyson Greengrass — standing a cart in the street for longer than necessary. Fined 2s.6d.

1892 — Alfred Tennyson Greengrass — allowing offensive matter to flow from his home into the street. Fined 10s.0d.

1894 — Thomas Fairfax Greengrass — leaving open a cellar door on the footpath to the discomfort of Sergeant O. Blaketon. Fined 15s.0d.

1897 — Jessica Flo Greengrass — shaking a doormat in the street after 8 a.m. Fined 2s.0d.

1900 — Five members of the Greengrass family were taken before the magistrates for lighting bonfires, letting off fireworks, placing streamers, flying kites, setting up market stalls and sundry other offences to the annoyance or obstruction of passers-by. In mitigation, members of the family said they had merely been celebrating the turn of the century. The magistrate was not amused — he was one of the persons who had been obstructed. Fines totalling £8.15s.0d. were imposed.

1909 — Ockleton Blatherwick Greengrass — riding a donkey on the footpath. Fined 5s.0d.

1924 — Claude Jeremiah Greengrass — riding on shafts of a cart. Fined 6d.

1936 — Claude Jeremiah Greengrass — furious driving of a cart. Fined 12s.6d.

1936 — Claude Jeremiah Greengrass — drunk in charge of a shotgun. Fined 15s.0d.

1936 — Claude Jeremiah Greengrass — keeping a dog without a licence. Fined 7s.6d.

1939 — Claude Jeremiah Greengrass — fortune-telling by using subtle crafts with intent to deceive members of HM Forces. Fined 10s.0d.

1939 — Claude Jeremiah Greengrass — being an idle and disorderly person, exposing his wounds to obtain alms. Fined 10s.0d.

Claude Jeremiah Greengrass then joined the army in 1939 and served until 1945 as a private, his main duty being to drive senior officers in official vehicles. His court martial records, if any, have not been made available, but he was prosecuted in the civilian courts for stealing petrol from military vehicles, selling petrol without a licence, acquiring petrol otherwise than from an authorised supplier and failing to accept petrol coupons at the time of supply of petrol. He was also convicted of selling food in air-raid shelters without a licence and making an unauthorised appeal for charitable donations.

He was found not guilty on each count. The chief prosecution witness was a Corporal Oscar Blaketon of the Royal Military Police who was criticised by the magistrates for bringing the cases to court without sufficient evidence.

Since leaving the army and settling down as a self-employed civilian rogue in Aidensfield, there has been constant conflict between Claude and ex-Corporal, later Constable and now Sergeant, Blaketon. Although Claude has appeared before the magistrates on many occasions, it is very rarely, if ever, that he is convicted.

Somehow, he manages to wriggle out of Blaketon's grasp. It is one of Sergeant Blaketon's great ambitions to secure a conviction against his old adversary. Some of their battles are recounted in my earlier *Constable* books but the saga continues in the following pages.

2. ANTECEDENT HISTORY OF CLAUDE JEREMIAH GREENGRASS

> ... antecedents are rum, Romanism, and rebellion.
> SAMUEL DICKINSON BURCHARD, 1812–91

When a person is found guilty before a court of law, a brief account of his or her life is presented to the court before sentence is pronounced. This is known as the defendant's "antecedents" and the document is prepared in advance by the police. Antecedents are not presented to the court when a defendant is found not guilty.

These antecedents are the combined product of the personal knowledge of police officers, the probation service and similar agencies, along with abstracts from any criminal record the accused might have accumulated and, of course, contributions from the accused. Comprising brief details of the accused's family background, career and criminal record, it enables the magistrates or judge to take into account the background of the guilty person before pronouncing sentence.

The rural beat constables who had worked at Aidensfield before my arrival had prepared useful antecedents for Claude Jeremiah Greengrass but throughout my period at Aidensfield, I had been able to provide details of my own.

For the benefit of readers who are new to the phenomenon known as Claude Jeremiah Greengrass, the following notes comprise his antecedent history.

Sergeant Blaketon was always of the opinion that this record was incomplete, firmly believing that Claude had committed many other offences for which he was never convicted. Nonetheless, this list has been compiled through privileged access to police records. Claude's pre-war convictions, collected while he was a juvenile, are given in the previous chapter.

The reference numbers indicate the year of his first recorded conviction in (a) West Riding of Yorkshire Criminal Record Office, (b) North Riding of Yorkshire Criminal Record Office and (c) the National Criminal Record Office at New Scotland Yard. In the latter case, only the more serious offences are recorded, and thus he did not commit a felony until 1940, his early offences being of a more petty nature, some while he was a juvenile. Records held at the West Yorkshire CRO were on a regional basis, whereas those in the North Riding were purely local.

CLAUDE JEREMIAH GREENGRASS

WRC No. 77645/24 NRC No. 39481/24 CRO No. 674438/40

Home Address: Hagg Bottom, Aidensfield (previously of Mirk House, Elsinby)

Date of Birth: 1st April 1911 Place of Birth: Aidensfield Hall

Mother: Anastasia Fabiola Greengrass (née Knapweed) — fortune-teller/peg-maker

Father: Thundercliffe Jasper Greengrass II — itinerant trader.

Claude Jeremiah Greengrass was born in the potting shed at Aidensfield Hall. Late one evening, his mother was in the shed for reasons which have never been established, and she was startled by a long-eared bat.

As a consequence, she gave premature birth to a son, her tenth child, and he was called Claude Jeremiah. Claude lived with his parents, his brothers and sisters at the family home, Mirk House, Elsinby. Conditions at home were described as chaotic.

At the age of five, he attended Elsinby Village School where his conduct was described as mercenary, apparently because he was always producing moneymaking schemes of doubtful legality. The punishment book shows that at the age of six he was disciplined for playing marbles for money or money's worth, using the other children's sweets as currency; Claude always beat the others and then sold the sweets back to the losers.

At eight, he organised a playground protection racket involving bicycle pumps and at ten, he was selling homemade wine to the five-year-olds. At eleven, he was caught stealing runner beans from the school garden, having sold them to the village shop and he was known to have supplied allegedly surplus school slates to a local builder for roofing purposes. He left school at the age of twelve and gained employment with the local blacksmith, pumping the bellows of the furnace and keeping sufficient water available to cool the newly made horseshoes. He was sacked for selling horseshoe nails to a racehorse owner.

By thirteen, he was self-employed, working from his parents' home and earning a living as an itinerant dealer and scrap-metal merchant. He sold old horseshoes to tourists as good-luck charms, fake horse brasses to public house licensees and false clay pipes to restaurant owners.

At fifteen he was selling water from Aidensfield Beck as a miracle cure to people suffering from facial spots. This enterprise ceased when he was prosecuted under s.72 of the newly introduced Public Health Act, 1925.

Upon the death of his parents in a train crash on Aidensfield Incline in 1927, Claude inherited the family home, none of his brothers and sisters wanting anything to do with the ramshackle old house, and he established himself there as a dealer in old metals and marine stores, specialising in unwanted milk churns, motor vehicle mudguards and anchors. He was awarded the necessary licence by the local authority, being licensed also as a hawker, pedlar, game dealer, pawnbroker, gravedigger and stallion keeper. He also held certificates enabling him to sweep chimneys and to ply for hire with horse-drawn and other non-mechanically propelled omnibuses.

He continued with this line of work throughout his life, mixing with people of doubtful integrity and engaging in schemes of suspect legality. In 1967, a freak whirlwind demolished his home and scattered his collection of hens and sheep, none of which were insured and none of his animals and birds were recovered. As rebuilding his home was impossible, he moved from Elsinby to Aidensfield where he managed to buy Hagg Bottom, Aidensfield, for cash. The house was previously owned by Ashfordly Estate; Lord Ashfordly wanted a quick sale but was understood to be somewhat dismayed when he discovered the identity of the purchaser. Claude's ability to find the cash (£4,000) was an event which attracted and continues to attract the interest of HM Inland Revenue.

For a man who claims never to have any money, it was an interesting purchase, but no fraud was disclosed nor did Claude's tax returns reveal any undeclared income.

As an HM Inspector of Taxes said at the time, "How he managed to find that sort of money baffles me."

Claude Jeremiah Greengrass continues to work as the village odd-job man, gravedigger, gardener, hedge-cutter and ditch-cleaner, along with any other paid employment he can find, while continuing to engage in various deals, including those involving scrap metal, old furniture, second-hand goods, second-hand cars and bankrupt stock.

While never likely to be a successful businessman, he does not commit serious crime but lingers on the edge of honest dealings. In spite of his ability to frustrate Sergeant Blaketon, he has several previous convictions including:

1952 — distilling whisky without an excise licence. Fined £20
1954 — discharging a firework on the street. Fined £2.10s.
1955 — no driving licence, tax or insurance for his van. Fined £15
1956 — exceeding the speed limit (licence endorsed). Fined £25
1957 — wilful obstruction of the highway with furniture. Fined £10

1958 — drunk while playing billiards. Fined £1
1960 — being found at night with his face blackened. Fined £3
1960 — brawling in a churchyard. Fined £7
1961 — maliciously abstracting electricity. Fined £7.10s.
1962 — receiving stolen property, i.e. manure. Fined £5
1962 — malicious damage to a rhubarb plant. Fined £2.10s.
1963 — knowingly uttering a counterfeit penny. Fined £5
1963 — trespassing in pursuit of conies. Fined £15
1963 — fishing without a licence. Fined £2
1963 — no dog licence. Fined 7s.6d.
1963 — trespassing upon the railway. Fined £2
1963 — pound breach. Fined £1.10s.
1963 — reversing an unnecessary distance. Fined £5

When I arrived at Aidensfield in the mid-1960s, I was instructed by Sergeant Blaketon to ensure that this list of convictions was extended; Blaketon's orders were that under no circumstances must I allow Claude Jeremiah Greengrass to escape the weight of English justice.

This book is therefore an account of some of the incidents which involved me and Aidensfield's resident rogue.

3. GREENGRASS ON WHEELS

> ... I cannot mind my wheel.
> WALTER SAVAGE LANDOR, 1775–1864

"The annual Bishops' Walk is a very prestigious affair, Rhea." Sergeant Blaketon was briefing me about the following Sunday's duty. "Very solemn too, as befits the office of those eminent gentlemen. You should be flattered that they have chosen Aidensfield Anglican Church for the Bishops' Walk service. It brings the cream of the English establishment into your village, Rhea, State and Church are one, as you know, the Conservative Party at prayer and all that. It's supposed to be a joyful occasion, however, because the idea of the walk is to give the senior clergy an opportunity to relax in the countryside, away from the cares of ecclesiastical office in a very informal atmosphere. Although it's called the Bishops' Walk, there are many participants who have not reached that eminent rank, ordinary reverends like vicars and canons. And a very few honoured guests not of the cloth."

"I know, Sergeant," I acknowledged, having performed this duty many times. The walk had originally been for bishops only, but small numbers had resulted in other clergymen and a very select number of guests being invited along. "They always enjoy it, Sergeant. It might appear solemn to us, but it's relaxing for them. And I must admit I've never seen so many happy smiling clergymen at one gathering. We usually get about two hundred and fifty of them and none has to preach a sermon, that must be a relief for starters!"

"The archbishop will be there too," Sergeant Blaketon reminded me. "So I want you to process with the walkers just to make sure everything is right on the day. No trouble, no barracking from silly youths or flak from insensitive tourists, no trouble from intolerant motorists — just keep things nice and calm, Rhea."

"We've never had trouble before, Sergeant."

"There's always a first time, Rhea. You must always expect the unexpected. And make sure no members of the public are admitted to the priory grounds until the reverends have gone. Remember, the police of Aidensfield and Ashfordly will be on show — we must do our best, we may need to seek Divine assistance one of these days. I might have to pray for sunshine if we hold an open day, for example."

"I understand, Sergeant," I assured him.

On the fourth Sunday of every July, Church of England bishops, canons and vicars from the north of England, with a few visitors from elsewhere, gathered at Aidensfield's parish church for a service at noon. Their host was a retired bishop, John Goodenough, who lived in the village and it was his fervent belief that all work and non-stop praying made bishops dull and boring. After the service, the clergymen, all clad in casual clothes, walked about three miles through beautiful countryside to the ruins of the twelfth century Briggsby Priory where they enjoyed an open-air picnic tea. The tea was always provided by the ladies of the parish, with considerable help from the ladies of the WI. There were sandwiches and cakes galore.

The priory, normally open to the public, was closed that afternoon so that the clergymen might enjoy a few moments of peace and tranquillity away from the public's gaze. After the picnic, a fleet of coaches would return them to

Aidensfield to collect their own transport for the return journey to their sees, palaces, dioceses, parishes and churches. I assured Sergeant Blaketon that I understood the need for discretion and sensitivity. I promised I would ensure the clergy had a wonderful day, at least so far as my responsibilities were concerned. What the Almighty had in store for them, however, remained unknown, although He was beseeched to produce a fine, warm and sunny day.

"I might just have a drive out there myself, to the priory, for the tea, Rhea," were Sergeant Blaketon's parting words. "I have a personal invitation. One of my former schoolmates is a bishop, you know; he rang to invite me along, he's coming to the walk. Very few non-clergy are invited, I might remind you. Anyway, they reckon my old friend's in line to be the next archbishop . . . Matthew Timothy's his name, surname Timothy that is. It'll be nice to see him again. That's two of us from Miss Stainton's class who have made a success of our lives. She always said me and him would get on, make our mark on the world."

And off he went in his polished black car leaving me to continue my patrol of Aidensfield. I had undertaken duties at the Bishops' Walk for several years and knew what was required, but I hoped that Sergeant Blaketon's presence and his esteem for an old schoolmate would not cause embarrassment. Sergeant Blaketon tended to be somewhat acquiescent and over-respectful in the presence of VIPs.

* * *

On the Saturday before the event, I had arranged to meet the organiser, John Goodenough, on the site; we always underwent that annual ritual in the grounds of the old priory for a final check of the plans, covering such matters as car-parking, the seating, access and egress arrangements especially in an emergency.

There were many on-site matters to check too. We repeated our visit every year because, from time to time, things did change. On this occasion, there was a new entrance to the grounds and I needed to see what effect it might have on the incoming and outgoing traffic. Our meeting was to be at two o'clock and I arrived a few minutes early. The priory was open to the public that afternoon and the custodian, aware of the reason for my visit, allowed me into the grounds without charge. John Goodenough arrived moments later and strode across the beautifully kept turf to shake my hand.

"Good of you to come, Constable." He was an affable and sturdy man in his early seventies who looked more like a retired farmer than an ex-bishop. He wore tweedy suits and brogue shoes and sported a round, red face with a perpetual smile beneath a monkish style of white haircut. "Well, I mustn't detain you longer than necessary so let's get started, shall we?"

"There's one change, Mr Goodenough," I announced before we moved away, pointing to the new gate. "They've installed a new gate over there, in place of the older wicket gate. It's wide enough to admit lorries now, which means the buses could reverse through here before collecting our walkers tomorrow. It'll get the buses off the road outside; the lane's very narrow as you know and a fleet of coaches parked outside will cause congestion. That was always a problem."

"Yes, I agree. I'll have them reverse into that space; there's room for several coaches in the grounds now. Actually," he beamed, "that new gate will improve the catering arrangements too. We've made some changes to the catering for tomorrow."

"You usually have a picnic tea done by the ladies of the parish?" I put to him.

"Yes, well we have had a rather nice offer this time. A range of dishes has been offered to us, hot and cold, with hot tea, soups, hotdogs even, from a mobile canteen."

"That sounds promising! I suppose a long walk in the fresh air will give your visitors an appetite?" I smiled.

"Yes, it does and, for some, buns and cakes are not sufficient, particularly as some have had a long journey to get here. This offer sounded infinitely better and I felt it was rather a good idea. That new gate means he can get his catering van right into the grounds, an ideal arrangement. The clergymen will pay for their own meals as I believe we can expect a very comprehensive menu."

I was aware of the use of the word "he" by John Goodenough, but couldn't think of any male caterers in this area who owned a custom-built mobile canteen.

"So, who is the caterer?" I asked.

"Oh, it's Mr Greengrass," he smiled at me. "You must know him."

"Claude Jeremiah Greengrass?" I couldn't believe my ears. "You mean he's doing your catering?"

"Yes, it appears he's bought a superb mobile canteen and is setting up in business. He's going to park it at local beauty spots in the summer, to cater for tourists, and hopes to visit the local agricultural shows and other places of public resort. Because I like to make use of local businesses, I felt he should be given this opportunity."

I didn't know what to say. The notion of a hotdog stall run by Claude Jeremiah Greengrass in the hallowed grounds of an ancient priory, even if it was for the benefit of some clerical gentlemen enhanced by the presence of an archbishop did not seem very wholesome. It was a bit like selling ice cream or fish and chips in church. I must admit I was trying to find reasons for suggesting the idea should be abandoned. Anything that Claude Jeremiah touched was usually a disaster, but what could go wrong in selling a range of food from a mobile canteen? The only likely disaster would be the quality of the fare on offer and if it fell below standard, the clergymen would not buy it. The problem would then be Claude's. It was hardly likely his presence would adversely affect anyone else, unless his food was poisonous.

"You've spoken to the custodian of the ruins?" I asked. "About permission to sell food here?"

"Oh, yes, and he's had words with his boss. Claude will have to pay a small rental for the privilege — only a pound on this occasion — and there is no other problem. As it is private property, he doesn't have to worry about licences or permission from the district council. It's not as if he's selling to the public from a public place — on this occasion, he will be selling to private individuals on private premises during what is a private occasion."

I had no wish to be unchristian towards Claude Jeremiah Greengrass but I did wonder what Sergeant Blaketon would make of the idea, especially if he was anxious to impress his old school friend. It was tempting to think that Claude would provide a useful service on the day, but the reality was that he'd probably sell unfit food, cold tea and greasy hotdogs. I told myself that it was no concern of mine — if these benevolent gentlemen wished to spend their money on Claude's version of wholesome food, then it was their decision. Yet I did find myself wanting to protect them against his wiles for there would surely be some drawbacks due to his presence. And should I alert Sergeant Blaketon to this unexpected development?

As we toured the superb grounds, no other problem presented itself — the seating arrangements had been finalised and we all thought the new gate was an asset especially for the admittance of any emergency vehicles, and for getting waiting vehicles off the road. But I knew it was also a liability because it had allowed access by Claude Jeremiah Greengrass and his new mobile canteen.

It was later that Saturday when I was patrolling the inns of my beat that I noticed Sergeant Blaketon's car parked in Ploatby High Street, awaiting my arrival. I eased my minivan to a stop and climbed out.

"All correct, Rhea?" Sergeant Blaketon emerged from his car and approached me.

"Yes, all correct, Sergeant."

We discussed the state of the local pubs that Saturday night but during my rounds I had not encountered anything or anyone that would provide cause for alarm.

"Greengrass out drinking, is he?" asked Blaketon.

"He's in the Hopbind at Elsinby tonight," I said, "having a pint or two with some scrappies. Probably fixing a deal of some kind."

"He's been quiet lately," was Blaketon's next comment. "Too quiet, if you ask me. He's plotting something. I'll bet."

This conversation provided me with the ideal opportunity to mention Claude's involvement in tomorrow's Bishops Walk. I knew I must inform Blaketon.

"Sergeant," I said, "just one thing. The refreshments at tomorrow's walk..."

"It's one of the reasons I'm going, Rhea!" he beamed. "Those Aidensfield women know how to lay on a good feed, believe me. Those ham sandwiches and homemade fruitcakes ... they're scrumptious!"

"Not this year, Sergeant," I said quietly. "There's been a change of plan."

"Really? Well, so long as the standards are maintained, I shall still look forward to my tea..."

"You might not, Sergeant," I heard myself say. "There's a mobile canteen this year, with hotdogs and soup and things ..."

"Really? Well, after a long walk, you can certainly work up an appetite..."

"It's Claude Jeremiah's canteen, Sergeant," I had to interrupt him. "Claude has set himself up with a mobile hotdog stall, and soup and things, and he's got permission to serve the bishops and clergymen tomorrow."

There followed an ominous silence and I could see Sergeant Blaketon's face going whiter and whiter as he struggled to come to terms with my news.

"Rhea, you are not serious! Tell me you are not serious about this?"

"John Goodenough has confirmed it, Sergeant," I said meekly. "The WI and parish ladies are not doing teas this time, Greengrass has got the job. There's a new gate at the priory, so he can get his canteen off the road and into the premises."

"Look, Rhea, you'll have to find a way of stopping him. I can't have this, not when my friend has invited me to the event as his special guest. Test his tyres, check his licence, find out if he's got a Refreshment House licence . . . anything . . . but just stop him from trading."

"I can't. Sergeant, I've gone into all that. It's a private party on private premises. The public won't be buying his food . . . besides, we can't stop him now, there's no time to find a substitute and, apart from that, I have no power to prevent him doing this."

"You disappoint me, Rhea!"

I tried to explain that the commissioning of Claude Jeremiah Greengrass to supply food and victuals at Briggsby Priory was nothing to do with the police service, and certainly no concern of mine. If John Goodenough had seen fit to employ Claude, it was good enough for me. In spite of Claude's dodgy reputation, I had no right to impose Sergeant Blaketon's opinions on others.

"If that man embarrasses me in front of my important friend, Rhea, you'll be working nights for a month!" were Blaketon's parting words.

* * *

The walk was very pleasant. The afternoon was dry and fine, if a little cool, but perfect for a mid-distance stroll by middle-aged and elderly clerical gentlemen.

On the walk from Aidensfield church to Briggsby Priory, I accompanied them on foot in my uniform, guiding passing cars past the procession and generally ensuring that no undue problems or traffic congestion occurred *en route*. On the way, I found myself chatting to several of the participants, including the archbishop, and realised they were charming, gentle people. Clearly, this day out was popular with them all; once they arrived at the priory, there would be a short service of prayers and hymns, and then they would break into informal groups to enjoy the tea which awaited them in the ruins. There was no doubt that some healthy appetites had developed. Sergeant Blaketon did not join the walk, but I knew he would arrive at the priory in due course, in the full splendour of his police uniform.

As the walkers approached the priory, I increased my pace and managed to get a hundred yards or so ahead of the procession; I wanted to open the new gate to admit them smoothly so they would not gather *en masse* around the entrance.

We did not want to cause a blockage of the road — a congregation of clergy milling around the narrow lane might cause an accident. But as I hurried towards the gate, I saw the ghastly psychedelic pink outline of a mobile canteen. A panel along one side of the rear section had been opened to form a counter, rather like an ice-cream van, and a small blackboard hanging on the outside bore a menu written in chalk. Black smoke was puffing from a tall tin chimney and the intense, but not very savoury, smell of cooked sausages and bacon wafted towards me on the gentle breeze.

I groaned at this vision of awfulness. Then, from inside, I was greeted by the familiar tones of Claude Jeremiah Greengrass who I saw was wearing a grubby white apron and a chef's hat. He beamed.

"How's this for an enterprise, eh, Constable? Got it for a song, I did, this old canteen . . . now, what can I get you?"

"Nothing just now, Claude," I said. "They're coming in for prayers and hymns before they eat . . ."

"Aye, well, I'm ready when they are. Full menu, good prices, fine food. You can't beat that combination, Constable. I wonder why I never thought of this before? Serving food's allus a good moneymaking business. Hot tea and coffee, cakes and scones, cooked foods galore . . . and I have a surprise for them vicars," He winked conspiratorially.

"Surprise?" I asked, not daring to ask what it was.

"Aye, it'll surprise and entertain 'em, Constable. It'll make their day memorable, I'd say. They'll talk about it for weeks afterwards; in fact it wouldn't surprise me if they asked me to attend their own church functions after this . . . You've got to have a gimmick, Constable."

"And when do you propose to deliver this surprise?" I wondered what sort of gimmick he was talking about.

"While they're all queuing up for their teas, I thought I'd put on a bit of entertainment."

"Entertainment?" I puzzled.

"There, Constable, I've said too much . . . Anyroad, I think it'll make my service unique in the annals of mobile canteens." He was clearly proud of his awful pink vehicle and just hoped he wasn't going to sing or play a loud radio. All these chaps wanted was a bit of peace and quiet among the historic ruins. "Now, if you'll allow me to prepare for the rush . . ." and he turned away to work on his counter.

The clergymen were now filtering into the grounds where the custodian had arranged chairs and benches in a haphazard fashion. As the men settled themselves down after the exertions of their walk, John Goodenough moved among them, checking that the more elderly were not suffering and that everyone had finally reached the ruins. None had been lost *en route*. Goodenough then asked them to bow their heads in prayer which he led, following which they sang a hymn without any musical accompaniment. Afterwards, the archbishop would say a few words. It was during this singing, that I noticed the arrival of Sergeant Blaketon. I went to meet him.

"Rhea!" was his first word as he pointed to the Greengrass canteen. "What is that monstrosity?"

"It's Claude's canteen," I said, as the hymn-singing filled the air around us. "And he's got a surprise for us, he says."

"I don't think I want to hear this, Rhea," he muttered. "Whoever let that man in here with that contraption needs his head looking at. Has anybody sampled the Greengrass wares, yet?"

"Not yet, Sergeant, they'll start when the service is over."

"Well, I'm not going to be first in the queue!" he muttered. "Let somebody else get poisoned! Come along, Rhea, let us patrol the grounds while our friends are getting themselves into a holy mood."

The hymn-singing and prayers lasted for about quarter of an hour during which time Blaketon and I executed a tour of the ruins. Throughout our stroll, he could not take his eyes off the eye-flickering pink shape that stood just inside the gate with dense black smoke issuing from its chimney. There was obviously a small stove inside the vehicle to provide the heat for cooking. In fact, the smell of cooking which now began to pervade the whole of the ruins was not too bad — it was appetising, in fact, and I found myself licking my lips in anticipation of a savoury sandwich of some kind. Then came the sound of the mighty *Amen* followed by the voice of John Goodenough exhorting his friends to queue at Claude's canteen for their teas.

"I'm going to find my friend," announced Blaketon. "I'll join him in the queue for tea." And off he went to find Bishop Matthew Timothy.

Claude had witnessed the move towards his canteen and started the engine of his vehicle; then Claude did something in the cab of his vehicle upon which the most awful noise sounded across the grounds. It was like a church organ which was badly out of tune and it was playing a ghastly version of "Abide with Me". I hurried towards the canteen and was first in the queue.

"Claude, what on earth is that racket?" I shouted at him above the noise.

"My organ," he beamed. "Look underneath . . ."

I looked under the vehicle and there somebody had fixed a range of organ pipes, they had been fitted to the floor of the vehicle, reaching from front to rear like several exhaust pipes and in the cab was a small keyboard which operated from a type used in a pianola.

"Good, eh?" he beamed. "I just flick a switch and the exhaust fumes are fed through those organ pipes . . . then I set the keyboard off and I've got organ music. I thought these chaps would appreciate that, eh, Mr Rhea? A grand bit of music, don't you think?"

The noise which came from the canteen sounded like a cross between a fairground organ and an out-of-tune bull bellowing its death throes, but the vicars, canons and bishops were heading towards it. And among them I saw Sergeant Blaketon and his friend, closely followed by the stately figure of the archbishop.

I ordered a hotdog, a slab of fruitcake and a mug of tea and turned around to find a place away from the awful din. I could see the embarrassment on Sergeant Blaketon's face as he joined his friend in the queue, but as I found a chair and settled down for my feed, I realised catastrophe had struck.

Something had gone wrong either with Claude's organ-pipe exhaust system or his stove, or both, as the entire canteen, along with dozens of people queuing for food, were enveloped in a cloud of dense black smoke. I could not see the canteen now, all I could see was a mass of thick smoke in the middle of which was Claude's canteen, an archbishop, an archbishop-in-waiting, several bishops, one police sergeant and dozens of vicars.

I heard them coughing; I saw Sergeant Blaketon rush out of the cloud doubled up as he coughed and coughed. He was trying to escape the black fumes which were making his eyes water and his lungs strive for fresh air. His face was black too, with panda-like white eyeholes . . .

I ran to the scene.

"Claude!" I shouted. "Switch the engine off!"

"I can't, summat's gone wrong with my stove. I can't see the key, I can't find my way into the cab," was the spluttered response. Then he rushed out of the rear door into the fresh air, his face black and his clothing covered with a thick black deposit. "Or mebbe one of my organ pipes is blocked and it's coming up from underneath . . . or summat . . ."

"Greengrass!" came the voice of Sergeant Blaketon. "I'll have you for this, so I will . . ."

"I do a good range of smoked bacon . . ." was Claude's weak response.

Actually, my food, which I had secured before the disaster, was quite tasty and I did enjoy it, but few of the others managed anything to eat that day. Eventually, I switched off the engine. The noise and the smoke faded away, but in the meantime, Claude's entire stock of food had become contaminated and several of the congregation were sitting down wiping tears from their eyes in the midst of blackened faces while coughing as if each had swallowed a swarm of flies. The archbishop did not look very happy at all. I think the chimney of the stove was the cause of the problem, but didn't wait to find out.

"If I see that monstrosity on the road, Greengrass," bellowed Sergeant Blaketon to the amusement of the vicars. "I'll have you. I'll bet you haven't a licence for music and I'll bet there's something in the Construction and Use Regulations and the Road Traffic Act which forbids organs being used under vans. I'll throw the book at you, Greengrass!"

"I think we should all sing, 'O Bread of Heaven'," grimaced Greengrass in the face of Blaketon's onslaught.

"Might I suggest 'Lo! He comes with clouds descending'?" chuckled Bishop Matthew Timothy at the side of Sergeant Blaketon.

* * *

Even in the 1960s, there were some 3,000 different rules and regulations governing the use of motor vehicles upon our roads. Generally speaking, the driving and use of motor vehicles on private premises did not, and does not, come within the scope of the road traffic laws and consequently police officers did not and do not concern themselves with such matters. Even in the mid-1960s, when a motor vehicle was upon a road, it was highly likely that either it or its driver was committing an offence of some kind. Few motorists can honestly say they have never committed a traffic offence; many have just been fortunate enough never to be caught or prosecuted.

One whose vehicles were always regarded by the police as "dodgy" was Claude Jeremiah Greengrass. It is fair to say that if one or other of his vehicles was stopped and checked, something illegal could be discovered, even without examining the vehicle in great detail. I had no wish to persecute the fellow, however, and found that a quiet word often resolved a problem. For example, I would ensure he taxed his vehicle, got it insured, made sure the brakes were up to standard or that the windscreen wipers worked properly — or made sure that he observed what other rule he was currently breaking. It was one of Claude's jokes that taxing and insuring an old vehicle didn't make it run any better and his chief concern was whether his old truck or van would reach its destination without breaking down. That was more important to him than any bits of official paper that might be required to keep it on the road.

If Claude did break the law, however, he often managed to do so in a quite spectacular way.

I was often reminded of the time he infringed Regulation 20 of the Motor Vehicles (Construction and Use) Regulations 1964 and, at the same time, managed to pose a question about interpretation of the provisions of section 77 of the Road Traffic Act 1960, as amended. In simple terms, he fitted the wrong sort of horn to his car and activated it as he was passing an elephant on the North York Moors. The consequence was that he collided with the elephant and ran off the road while the elephant escaped unscathed.

The law about horns on cars, officially known as audible warning instruments, said that no motor vehicle, other than those used by the emergency services, should be fitted with a bell, gong, siren or two-tone horn. The logic for this was simple — these instruments were all designed to warn the public of the urgent approach of an emergency vehicle of some kind. Claude Jeremiah Greengrass, however, managed to acquire an audible warning instrument for his old pickup truck and it played the first few bars of "Colonel Bogey", the well-known military march written by K.J. Alford. He drove through Aidensfield playing his tune to the delight of the children and the annoyance of residents but always managed to avoid me. It was sometime before I learned of the presence of the Greengrass audible warning instrument — and it was Sergeant Blaketon who told me.

"Tell that man Greengrass to get rid of that horn, Rhea, its illegal. He blew it in Ashfordly High Street this morning and made me drop the eggs I'd bought."

"I've never heard it, Sergeant," I had to admit.

"It plays 'Colonel Bogey', Rhea, bloody cheeky if you ask me, an insult to upright people, playing that in a street or public place. People never sing the proper words when they hear it . . . you know what they sang to it in *The Bridge on the River Kwai* . . ."

"I'll have words with him, Sergeant."

"You'll do more than that, Rhea, you'll order him to have it removed, otherwise he goes to court."

I found Claude at his ramshackle ranch where he was feeding his hens. At my approach, he grinned and said, "Let me guess, Constable, you've been sent to tell me to get rid of my new horn?"

"You made Sergeant Blaketon drop his eggs this morning." I had to smile at my vision of that incident. "Blasting him from behind with 'Colonel Bogey' isn't exactly a relaxing trick. You know it's illegal, a horn of that kind."

"No it's not, Constable." He blinked furiously at me, grinning at the same time. "I checked. Two-tone horns are illegal, mine's not a two-tone horn. It's a multi-tone horn; there's more than two notes and the suppliers told me they'd carried out their own research into the law. It's not illegal."

When I checked the wording of the relevant regulation, I discovered he was right. Multi-tone horns were not unlawful; even though this was probably an oversight by the parliamentary draughtsmen, the definition of a two-tone horn (which produces a sound alternating at regular intervals between two fixed notes) did not include Claude's device.

It meant I could not forbid him to use it, and it meant he was not committing a road traffic offence. His horn was beyond the law.

Sergeant Blaketon was furious. "Get him for something else then, Rhea; he must be offending with that rubbishy old truck of his."

But I had no wish to persecute poor old Claude; if he was not committing an offence against the traffic laws, I must not let personal opinions dictate to me or compel me to enforce non-existent laws. In all conscience, I could not compel him to remove the noisy horn if he was not breaking the law — and even if the residents of Aidensfield grumbled at his persistence in playing "Colonel Bogey" as he motored through the village. But our salvation came with the Aidensfield Ambulation.

This was an annual event held on the third Sunday of March, the idea being that the people of Aidensfield trekked from the Aidensfield War Memorial to Crampton Ings, a local nature reserve where they had a picnic. Crampton Ings was about seven miles away and the purpose was to trek between the two places without the use of mechanically propelled transport. No motorcycles, cars, vans, steam rollers, traction engines or anything containing an engine must be used — the trip had to be completed on foot, although non-mechanically propelled aids like roller skates, horses and bicycles could be used. The Ambulation was to raise funds for local charities and it was always well supported.

On the day in question, three of the local lads decided to hire an elephant from a local zoo and they would complete the Aidensfield Ambulation upon the elephant whose name was Septimus.

As this was quite within the rules no one objected and so Septimus started the stroll with one of his three hirers on board. As elephant and handlers were trekking across Crampton Heights, an open stretch of elevated moorland, it transpired that Claude Jeremiah Greengrass was chugging along the same road with a load of scrap metal in his old pickup truck.

Claude, not the wisest of people on occasions, decided to entertain Septimus and friends with a tune on his multi-tone audible warning instrument. Claude slowed down behind the elephant and reduced his speed to a crawl to give him the full benefit of the horn; as he approached the rear of the huge beast, therefore, the air was rent with the tinny tones of the music of "Colonel Bogey".

Septimus was quite startled by the sudden din close to his rear end and lashed out with one of his powerful rear legs. He kicked the front wheel of Claude's truck just as Claude was beginning to accelerate past, but the kick turned the wheels to their right and jerked the steering wheel out of Claude's hands. The outcome was that Claude found himself roaring off the road as he grappled with the spinning steering wheel and fought to find the brakes in the midst of his frustration, but he was too late. His loaded truck careered off the road and nose-dived into a ditch, flinging Claude clear before the load of scrap metal crushed the cab. Claude scrambled up to the highway, waving his fist and shouting, "I'll have you for this, I'll have the police on you . . ."

"Shall we get Septimus to drag your truck out, Claude?" grinned one of the lads.

"You'll not let that monster anywhere near my truck!" snarled Claude. "That's dangerous driving, dangerous driving of an elephant by my standards . . ."

Having realised that Claude was unhurt, the lads continued on their way as Claude struggled back to the village to call on me.

"I've come to report an accident," he said, and he then outlined the incident.

"It's not a reportable accident, Claude," I smiled at him. "The police have no jurisdiction over it. An elephant is not classified as an animal in British road traffic law."

"What do you mean? Not an animal?"

"So far as our traffic laws are concerned, accidents involving animals apply only to dogs, goats, cattle, horses, asses, mules, pigs and sheep. Not cats, hens, foxes, rabbits, badgers, crocodiles, zebras, elephants or anything else. Just those domestic animals I've mentioned."

"You mean there's nothing I can do about it?"

"No. Claude, nothing, unless you have words with your insurance man. Only he can tell you if you're insured for collisions with, or kicks from, elephants. And you might find that you were at fault, scaring the beast with 'Colonel Bogey'!"

"That's not illegal, Constable, and you know it."

"Neither is colliding with an elephant, Claude. And now you know that!"

Later, I learned that when the old truck was dragged from the ditch by a breakdown vehicle, it was not too badly damaged. Although the load had shifted and crushed the cab, a new cab could be easily fitted but there was one saving grace — the crash rendered the horn unusable. "Colonel Bogey" disappeared from Aidensfield, thanks to a well-aimed kick from Septimus the elephant.

Sometime later, the law on audible warning instruments was altered — it became illegal to fit multi-tone horns to motor vehicles but in the UK, it is still not a reportable traffic accident if your vehicle collides with an elephant.

4. GREENGRASS AT THE FAIR

He haunts wakes, fairs, and bear baitings.
WILLIAM SHAKESPEARE, 1564–1616

The Aidensfield annual Church Fête and Fair was, by local standards, an impressive and most enjoyable occasion. The fête and fair committee was allowed the use of a level field with good vehicular access on the edge of the village, courtesy of a local farmer, and important contacts within the village community meant that a modest selection of professional fairground entertainments was made available. There were dodgem cars, for example, a big dipper, shooting galleries, a bingo stall, an amusement arcade with machines and various other attractions which had been provided by Giovanni Morrelini, the amusement arcade king whose kingdom stretched along the seafront at Strensford. He lived in Aidensfield, however, away from the hustle and bustle of that busy seaside resort. He was always very supportive of village functions, on this occasion allowing the village to make use of part of his travelling fair. He shared any profits with the village charities, and his generosity was always appreciated.

The fête and fair ran for two days on a weekend in mid-August when, in addition to Morrelini's equipment and personnel, the local people staged their own entertainments. There was, quite literally, all the fun of the fair from three-legged races to guessing the weight of a sheep or a fruit-cake. There were balloon races for the children and, for the adults, estimating the number of miles a Morris 1000 would run on a tankful of petrol or how many dried peas there were in a pint-sized milk bottle. Teas and refreshments were provided by the ladies of Aidensfield, and George from the pub ran a beer tent with hot pies and soup. It was always a happy occasion.

As the village constable, my part was to ensure that traffic moved freely through Aidensfield during the fair, that no obstruction was caused, no litter was dropped in the village and no trouble was caused in the local inns by boisterous youths anxious to impress giddy young girls. There was an emergency tent on the site to cater for lost property and lost children as well as administering first aid and providing information for those who made enquiries. Occupants of the tent, all volunteers, were expected to know everything from the time of the last bus to Ashfordly to the names of the winners of every competition. The tent was also used by those who wished to complain to the fête secretary for any reason — someone always complained, either about car-parking, flies, mud on their shoes or cold tea. Most complaints were frivolous and unnecessary but some people love to complain — there are lists of petty complainers in most police stations but church fêtes are no exception to the rule that you can't please all the people all the time.

The police were expected to use that tent too. It was probably the busiest place on the site — it was astonishing the things that could go wrong on a day's outing, especially with children. In addition, I had to patrol the fairground to ensure that the law was not broken.

I had to make sure that pickpockets were not operating among the crowds and that everyone had a pleasant, crime-free time. Normally, I did not experience problems at the fair: it was always well organised and well attended; most country people are sensible, calm and well behaved. Even rural youngsters and teenagers display a modicum of common sense and courtesy. The occasion was always a thoroughly decent and happy one with most of the participants winning modest prizes in either the tombola, raffle or on-going competitions. Things like the shooting ranges, coconut shies, roll the pennies and similar games of skill always produced a wide range of happy winners.

At least, that was the situation until the year that Rebus the Great arrived.

Because I was not a member of the organising committee, I had no part in the choice of participating acts. I had no idea of the part to be played by Rebus the Great, nor did I know who sheltered beneath that odd alias. I became aware of his presence when I saw his tent pitched beside that of Gipsy Rose Lee. The tent of Rebus the Great was a tall, narrow structure, rather like a miniature lighthouse with the top half chopped off. It had a shallow pointed roof with a pennant flying from the top and I was reminded of the kind of tent used by the Knights Templar when knights were bold, fought good fights and rescued fair maidens from fates worse than being eaten by fire-breathing dragons.

The tent of Rebus the Great was brightly adorned with broad red and white stripes and outside was a large handwritten notice saying, *Pit Your Wits Against Rebus the Great. Spend five shillings to win £5. Satisfaction Guaranteed.* A smaller notice added, *No person may have more than one attempt* and at the bottom was a sign pointing towards the dark, windowless interior of the tent. Inside, as the flap was opened, there was a small table bearing a candle in a bottle; there was one chair before it and another behind for the use of Rebus the Great as he sat face to face with his client. He was heavily dressed in brightly coloured robes, golden shoes with turned-up points and a golden face mask, a real mystery man from the East.

I did not enter that tent; I had no wish to tempt my fortune by spending five shillings upon a solo effort to win a fiver. I suppose it was my inbred police caution which told me that there was probably a bit of innocent (or not-so-innocent) trickery here. It was the sort of jiggery-pokery one could accept in this situation. I'd heard that the sights of some fairground rifles were slightly off true so that few marksmen could hit a target; some said the coconuts were glued to their stands so they could not be dislodged; while things like miniature mobile cranes would never lift anything heavier than a feather, let alone a bar of chocolate or a bag of pennies. The fun of the fair invariably involved a spot of acceptable deception. But not for me.

Perhaps I should have taken more notice of the tent of Rebus the Great when I noticed the furtive appearance of the snout of a grey dog, followed by a shout of "Alfred, get under that table and sit down!" That should have told me the identity of Rebus the Great, but at that innocent stage, I just thought that Claude Jeremiah Greengrass's flea-ridden dog had accompanied Claude into the tent while Claude was attempting to win a small fortune.

It never occurred to me that Claude was in fact Rebus the Great. Had that knowledge presented itself to me, I should have entered the tent to discover what devious scheme he was plotting. Blissfully unaware of the moneymaking drama going on within the little tent, therefore, I performed my patrols at the fête and was pleased that everything went very smoothly. Then I began to hear people talking; they weren't exactly grumbling and there was no official complaint, but in the queue for tea, in the queue for the loo and the queue for ice cream, I heard people talking about Rebus the Great. The chatter revealed that not one person had won the expected £5. On the other hand, all had been very very close to winning; by the narrowest of margins, they had almost won and all had believed themselves very capable of completing the minor task set by Rebus the Great but none had succeeded in winning anything. And there was no second chance. No one was allowed a second go.

As I listened to their chatter, I discovered how he operated.

It seemed that the client entered the tent and was confronted by Rebus the magician who held a pack of playing cards. The client paid his or her five shillings, whereupon Rebus the Great cut the pack into two sections. He then turned over the card on top of the lower section. It was always the ace of diamonds. That charade was done to prove that the ace of diamonds was indeed within the pack. The pack was then reassembled and cut several times to mix the cards, always with the client being asked to watch carefully in an attempt to follow the position of the ace of diamonds. The client had to pay five shillings which allowed only one cut of the cards. The client then personally cut the deck. If he or she cut it so that the ace of diamonds was on the bottom of the section in their hands, i.e. the cards they had lifted from the pack on the table, they won £5. There was no second chance. At that stage, Rebus the Great turned over the next card, the one sitting on top of the lower half, and it was always the ace of diamonds. That proved it was still in the pack and it meant that the punter had missed winning £5 by the narrowest of margins. Its position meant that out of an entire pack of fifty-two cards, the client had missed the ace of diamonds by the thickness of just one playing card. Word had got around that everyone was just missing the winning card which meant they should be very capable of finding it with a little more practice — but Rebus the Great did not allow anyone a second chance. Even so, a queue developed outside his premises; he was making a small fortune because people were talking about the challenge. All had been so very close to winning . . . and now others were paying for that opportunity, yet none emerged a winner. Rebus didn't pay anyone.

The logic was that if other people had been so close to winning, then anyone might win the prize. Rebus the Great was obviously a student of human nature and he was making a very useful sum of money. I began to wonder how much he would donate to village charities. As I listened to several accounts of this piece of trickery, I began to realise how the trick was performed — I had done it myself, during my card-conjuring days. I thought I would pay a visit to Rebus the Great. As I was musing upon the ethics of his performance, however, and trying to decide whether or not I should reveal his trickery to the world, Sergeant Blaketon arrived.

The end of the fête was rapidly approaching and he had come to see how things had progressed. He spotted me holding a cup of tea and so I organised one for him; my resolve to visit Rebus the Great was therefore abandoned, at least temporarily. By the time I had discussed things with Blaketon, Rebus would probably have left his tent, packed his deck of cards and left with a small fortune.

"All correct, Sergeant," I produced the expected response to his arrival.

"A nicely organised event, Rhea." He sounded very pleased. We chatted for a while, and then he asked, "So, where's Greengrass?"

"I haven't seen him, Sergeant," I admitted. "I think he's not far away, though, I saw his dog here earlier. You'd never get Alfred wandering around this place without his lord and master."

"Well, so long as his dog is wearing a collar and Greengrass has got a licence for the animal, there is no reason why he should not bring that hound here. Now, Rhea, I think I will show the great British public of Aidensfield that the face of the police service is human," Blaketon announced, after he had enjoyed several ham sandwiches and cakes and drunk umpteen cups of tea. "I'll have a potter around, I might just try one or two of the sideshows. And if Greengrass is here, I'll make sure he's not causing trouble! You might do likewise!"

"Very good, Sergeant," and off he went.

It would be about quarter of an hour later, as I was undertaking a gentle perambulation around the sideshows, that I noticed Sergeant Blaketon duck into the tent of Rebus the Great.

The queue had dwindled and so the bold sergeant, resplendent in his uniform, had taken the opportunity to attempt to win a crisp fiver. But as the sergeant entered the tent, I noticed the nose of Alfred the lurcher peeping out from beneath the canvas to the left of the opening; he was sniffing the atmosphere and, having been cooped up all day in that airless place, was doubtless savouring the fresh moorland air, along with the scents of lady dogs or hotdogs. It was at that stage that I realised the identity of Rebus the Great. And his latest client was none other than Sergeant Oscar Blaketon. This could be interesting.

Fully realising how Claude Jeremiah was performing his ace of diamonds trick, I decided to hang about outside, just in case I was needed to quell a breach of the peace. I wasn't sure how knowledgeable Sergeant Blaketon was about trick packs of cards, card sharping or people's ability to manipulate packs of playing cards, although I was perfectly aware of his skill in interpreting the wiles of Claude Jeremiah Greengrass.

As I hung around the tent, its door now closed to conceal the client from the outside world, I heard Blaketon's voice rise above the noise of the fair as he shouted, "It's you, Greengrass! I might have known . . . cheating and frauding as usual . . . I want my money back!"

"It was just a bit of fun, Sergeant," responded the quiet voice of Claude. "I mean, it's all for charity, good causes . . ."

"Good causes? Greengrass causes more like! Greengrass! You're a cheat . . . I want you to repay all that money and give it to the show secretary, in my presence . . ."

And with that, the door of the tent burst open and out bolted Sergeant Blaketon with a half-nelson grip on the arm of Rebus the Great in his gaudy red silk robes and a golden mask. Blaketon ripped off the mask to reveal the unmistakable features of Claude Jeremiah Greengrass. Then he saw me.

"Rhea, this man is a cheat and a rogue and a vagabond and a card-sharping charlatan . . ."

"You mean you didn't win a fiver, Sarge?" I grinned.

"Win a fiver, Rhea? Nobody can win a fiver with this pack of cards. It's a trick pack."

"I know, Sergeant. I know how it works . . . it's an old conjuring trick, you see, and . . ."

"You mean you knew what was going on? That you are party to this deception, Rhea? That's a fine admission, coming from an officer of the law!"

I tried to explain that I had only just come to appreciate what Rebus the Great, alias Claude Jeremiah Greengrass, had been doing, and that it was all being done for charity, but Blaketon was in no mood for listening. He released his hold on Claude and made him turn out his pockets as Alfred and a growing crowd of observers gathered. Claude had pockets full of money and Sergeant Blaketon made him place every penny on the grass before him.

"That's my own money, Mr Blaketon," protested Claude. "I mean, that in my back pocket is nowt to do with this fair . . ."

"I don't believe you Greengrass. Now, all this money goes to charity, the lot. That is your punishment for cheating."

"Aye, well, I mean, I was going to hand it over," blinked the embarrassed Claude. "I need some to pay my tent rent."

"You'll have to find it from somewhere else, Greengrass!" snapped the angry sergeant. "Now, give me that pack of cards."

"A magician never shows how he does his tricks, Sergeant. It's sacred, Magic Circle, you know, we've rules about not revealing trade secrets."

"Cards, Greengrass!" And he held out his hand for Claude's magic pack. Reluctantly, he handed them to Sergeant Blaketon who tossed them across to me.

"Rhea," he said, "you know how the trick works, please explain to these good people."

I eased the pack of cards from their packet and showed them to the crowd, explaining that they had all the appearances of a genuine pack of playing cards. But they were stacked so that every second card was an ace of diamonds. The pack consisted of twenty-six aces of diamonds, all with the same coloured backs on them, and twenty-six mixed cards with other face values. And every ace of diamonds had been cut a fraction shorter in length than the other cards. This meant that if anyone cut the pack in the normal way (and the conjurer ensured they did cut it the normal way by holding the cards towards them while gripping the sides) they would always break the pack at one of the normal cards. The bottom card of the top half of the cut pack would always be an ordinary card, not the ace of diamonds. But the one below it would be an ace of diamonds. That was the reason why no one had a second opportunity to pick a card — anyone with half a brain would quickly realise that the pack was fixed. And, preying on the desire of the punters to win something worthwhile, Claude knew they would talk about just missing the prize — and so persuade others to have a go. Using the cards as a magician would, I explained the trick to them and then, quite suddenly, everyone began to boo Claude.

He began to slink away, but I called, "Claude, your cards. You might need them again."

"You keep 'em," he muttered. "You do it next time . . ."

"Ladies and gentlemen," I called to the crowd, "Claude has donated all his takings to charity . . . a very noble effort, I feel." Suddenly the boos turned to applause and Claude halted to acknowledge the cheers. "You are very charitable today," I praised the people and then, with the crowd in a good mood once more, they began to disperse. The show was over. Justice had been done.

"You didn't give me change for my pound, Greengrass," snarled Blaketon when the crowd were moving away. "I paid a pound for a five-bob gamble, and you said you had no change . . ."

"It's gone to charity now, Mr Blaketon," grinned Claude. "I'm sure you can afford fifteen shillings for charity. I've donated a lot more I'll have you know. Now, I have another trick you might like to see . . . cups and balls, it is. All you have to do is work out which cup covers the white ball . . ."

"Greengrass, if I hear one more suggestion from you, I'll nick you and confiscate your balls!"

* * *

I had similar problems with Greengrass at another gala in Aidensfield. This one was being run for the benefit of the Red Cross and it was in the spacious grounds of Aidensfield Manor, courtesy of Mr and Mrs Barraclough. Although on a much smaller scale than the village fête and fair, many of the villagers had volunteered to provide stalls and entertainments. Among them was Claude Jeremiah Greengrass. He said he would run the coconut shy.

The gala, at which the Ashfordly Brass Band was playing, was on a Saturday in September and the weather was gorgeous. Bright, warm and sunny, it was the perfect day for such an event and the villagers responded wholeheartedly by bringing their friends and families and encouraging visits from neighbouring communities. There were watery games like ducking for apples and throwing wet sponges at a volunteer whose head was fastened in a frame, sports events for children and parents, stalls selling everything from local handicrafts to cakes by way of second-hand crockery to knitwear. Tests of skill were included. There was an air rifle stall where the contestants had to hit moving ducks and knock them down, and another where competitors had to throw darts at a dartboard, with those scoring more than a hundred with three shots winning a box of chocolates. There were the inevitable cakes and teas, a stall staffed by Red Cross volunteers and a host of other interesting sights. And there was the coconut shy.

It was my day off on this occasion and I was attending the gala with Mary and the family; the children loved every moment and ran about excitedly, wanting to try everything, eat everything and win everything. We gave them some cash to spend and allowed them to select their own events. As they did this, I noticed Claude at his stall and decided to try and win a coconut. The cost was sixpence for three attempts.

Having paid my sixpence, I would receive three hard wooden balls and the idea was to knock the coconuts off their stands at the far end of the tent. There was a counter behind which Claude stood and this provided a suitable barrier against those who might get too close. You stood at the counter and threw from the public side of it; the players could keep every coconut they dislodged.

"Now then, Mr Rhea," blinked Claude when he noticed my approach. "You've come to try your hand, have you?"

"I thought I would test my old skills," I laughed. "I'm a fairish bowler at cricket and can usually hit the stumps with a throw-in."

"Aye, well, it's different in these conditions, you know." He was blinking furiously as he handed me the three balls. "No wind to help your throw, not much daylight at yon end of the tent, and a small target . . . I mean to say them coconuts aren't very big, not like balloons."

I looked at the array of coconuts. They were at the distant end of Claude's long tent, in semi-darkness, and all were perched in a shallow bowl on top of a pole, there was a row of twelve coconuts — Claude was offering a discount for twelve balls. One and sixpence for twelve balls was the offer, the prize being the opportunity to win a dozen coconuts if every throw scored. I settled for three balls and handed over my sixpence.

"They're funny looking coconuts, Claude," I peered into the gloom. "I haven't seen coconuts shaped like that, Claude. Genuine, are they?"

He blinked even more furiously. "Aye, they are. Specials, all the way from the tropics, Malabar and the West Indies no less. Specially grown coconuts from coconut-shy-producing trees, specially imported for throwing balls at. Or missing with balls as the case may be. Mind you, they taste good. Full of creamy milk, they are, better than a tin of condensed milk from contented cows, I'd say. And the flesh . . . well, you'll never taste anything better, Mr Rhea. Mark my words. Them who can knock one of my coconuts off are in for a treat."

"Are they ripe?" I asked because they had a distinct greenish colour with yellowish markings showing through, although there were tufts of ginger hair protruding from the tops. It was the sort of hair one would expect on a coconut.

"Ripe? Of course they're ripe. You're doubting me already, Constable! Them coconuts is as ripe as they ever will be," blinked Claude. "Now look, this is a bit of fun. You're not on duty now, you've got your balls, if you'll pardon the expression, so see if you can knock a coconut off; if you can, it's yours."

Concentrating upon my throw, I missed with the first two balls, but the third struck one of the coconuts firmly in the centre of its widest part. I felt there was power behind my throw, certainly enough to knock the coconut from its perch, but the coconut did not budge. On top of that, the impact made a peculiar sound — I had always thought coconut shells were hard and that they would produce a wooden sort of noise when struck with a wooden ball. But this didn't; it was a duller sound. Maybe unripe coconuts had softer shells? It wasn't all that important, but I was surprised at this outcome — a firm hit of that kind would normally have dislodged the coconut.

"Are your coconuts glued to their bases, Claude?" I asked.

"Of course not! I'll not have you casting doubts on my integrity, Constable," he blinked. "It's just that you didn't hit it right. Hit it right and it'll fall off, then it's yours. No sour grapes, Constable, be a sportsman, accept defeat graciously. The umpire's decision is final, and I'm the umpire."

Not having any desire to appear unsporting, ungracious or even slightly suspicious about Claude's enterprise, especially as a small queue had formed behind me, I decided against having any further shies at the array of Greengrass coconuts and turned away. It would be about half an hour later, as I was trying to locate Mary and the children, when I encountered Joe Steel. Joe, a silver-haired man in his early sixties, owned the village shop in Aidensfield which also served as the post office, and he was acting as a kind of unofficial master of ceremonies for the gala. He was making sure everything was properly arranged; I saw him ask a motorist to move his car because it was obstructing the entrance and on another occasion, he helped a lady in a wheelchair to negotiate the doorway to one of the displays.

"Hello, Nick," he smiled. "Enjoying yourself?"

"Yes thanks, Joe. I've got Mary and the children here somewhere, they're having a fine time."

"Tell them not to have a go at Claude's coconuts," he grinned. "They'd be wasting their money."

I didn't tell him I had wasted a small sum on Claude's stall, but asked, "Why's that, Joe?"

"Those coconuts of his, well, they're not coconuts. They're turnips!"

"You're joking!" I cried. "Of all the nerve! Turnips? That man gets worse!"

"Well, to give him his due, he did try to buy some coconuts off me, but I only had one. Claude bought that, and then asked for a sack of turnips. He'd got some supports for his coconuts, and found that if he shaved a bit off the bottom of a turnip, it would fit snugly into the space. They're fitted into those stands, Nick, made to measure in fact. Mind, you'll never knock them out, they're too firmly wedged in.

"I thought they didn't look very realistic," I had to admit. "But they do have bits of coconut fibre on them . . ."

"From one of Claude's old coconut mats, he's stuck the hairs on to make 'em look reasonably like coconuts . . . in the dark, it's hard to tell the difference."

"So nobody is likely to knock one off its perch, eh?"

"And if anybody does, Claude does have one coconut to give away, he's keeping that out of sight, just in case! And he is giving the takings to the Red Cross, Nick, I have checked that with him, just to be sure about his motives!"

"It would be nice to play a joke on him, Joe," I smiled.

"It would have to be right at the end of the gala, Nick, he's making good money for the Red Cross just now."

"I'll give it some thought," I mused as I heard Mary's voice behind me. I turned away to greet the children who had arms full of candy floss, soft toys and colouring books they had either won or purchased.

"They want to go into the playground now," smiled Mary. "There's a chute and some high swings."

So off we went.

It was in the playground that an idea came to me. Helping his young daughter to use a children's swing was Danny Shipley; Danny was a van driver who worked for a department store in Ashfordly. He lived in Aidensfield and was a regular in George's pub where his skill with darts was almost legendary. When he was on form, he was unbeatable, he was a true maestro of the dartboard. He could beat any opponent in any of the many variations of darts games and it was said he had once thrown six arrows into the bull, one after the other, so that all six were grouped in that small space. I knew that he always carried a set of arrows, as he called his darts, and decided to ask him a favour.

"What I want you to do, Danny," I said, "is to have a go at Claude's coconut shy, but use your arrows instead of the wooden balls."

"I'd damage the tips, Nick," he said. "They'd bounce off coconut shells and I'd ruin them."

"He's using turnips instead of coconuts," I told Danny. "I want him exposed — I thought if you threw your darts at them, they'd stick into the flesh and the game would be up!"

"I can borrow some arrows from the dartboard stall," he grinned. "They'll be good enough for this job. I thought those coconuts didn't look too realistic, but you don't like to make a fuss, do you?"

"That's what Claude is relying on," I smiled. "Folks not making a fuss. He's had his fun with us, now we can have a bit of fun at his expense."

Danny spread news of his forthcoming throws on the coconut shy among his pals and as the gala was drawing to a close, they all arrived at Claude's stall. I was there too, to watch the fun. One or two of Danny's mates paid their sixpence for three balls and flung them at the coconuts with all the power they could muster. Several struck home with solid thwacks, but none of the coconuts was dislodged. Now, of course, we all knew why.

"Come on you lot!" Claude shouted. "It's closing time, everybody else is packing up . . . I can't hang around here all day!"

"There's just me, Claude," said Danny stepping forward. "I'm the last."

He paid one and sixpence for the opportunity to throw at all twelve of the solidly situated "coconuts" as Claude was saying, "Nobody's knocked one off yet, Danny . . ."

"I thought I'd use my own missiles, Claude," beamed Danny. "There's nothing in the rules about having to use those wooden balls, is there?"

"Well, I don't know about that, Danny," blinked Claude. "I mean, well, everybody else has used the balls . . ."

"It'll be harder for me, Claude," and Danny pulled a set of arrows from his rear pocket. "The points of my arrows are much smaller than those balls."

"Darts? You can't use darts on a coconut shy! Especially not you . . . !"

"They're not coconuts, Claude," laughed Danny. "They're turnips, and there's nowt about not using arrows on a turnip shy," and with that he threw the first three darts towards their targets. Each struck home. Each sank deeply into the turnip as Danny pulled more darts from his pocket and, with lightning movements, buried them all in the turnips. Very soon every turnip was fletched with a clutch of arrows all buried up to the butt in the flesh of the vegetable. Chunks of turnip had flown far and wide during the onslaught and by the time Danny had completed his work, each of the target turnips was a sorry sight.

Claude stood by in silence, blinking his embarrassment at the laughing crowd and saying, "Well, they looked like coconuts and they did have a bit of coconut matting on top and I have one to give away . . . you can have it, Danny, I reckon you've won."

"Claude, you're an old cheat!" smiled Danny. "Now, how much have you made for the Red Cross, eh?"

"Aye, well, I dunno, I haven't counted up yet, I mean, there's my expenses, you know."

"Twelve turnips and a coconut," laughed Danny, holding out his hands. "Come on, Claude, empty your pockets."

And for the second time that year, Claude Jeremiah Greengrass had to empty all his pockets for charity. From the heap of cash which appeared on the counter of his stall, it seemed he had done well for the Red Cross.

"I wonder if anybody wants to buy some turnips?" he asked me when everyone had gone.

"Not after the treatment they've had, Claude, they look like mashed turnips now. But I'll buy the coconut."

"You will, Mr Rhea?" his face brightened at the news.

"My kids will love it. I can always tell them I won it fair and square on your coconut shy!" I teased him. "And I'll give the money for it to the gala secretary," I added as Claude's smile faded.

* * *

Another of Claude's schemes was doomed to failure and it owed just a little to the fairgrounds of the area. Claude had seen Gypsy Rose Lee forecasting people's lives and realised that gullible folks were easily persuaded to part with their hard-earned cash if they believed they were learning something to their advantage. The trick was to make them believe that what they were hearing was true which, in his case, meant concealing his real identity. I must admit I had no idea of his scheme until things began to grow repeatedly wrong. My knowledge of Claude's grand plan, albeit not realising at the time that Claude was the perpetrator, came to light when I paid a visit to Jack Earnshaw of High Toft Farm which was a modest spread on the moors above Aidensfield. It was a blustery March day and the heights bore a covering of snow, an overnight fall which had surprised even the professional weather forecasters. Added to this, there was an extremely chill wind from the north.

"I'd just put my lambs out," grumbled Jack, as we sat at his kitchen table enjoying a mug of hot tea and a scone. "I relied on that chap who writes for the paper — he said this week would be mild and dry with sunshine and clear skies so I thought I'd turn my flock out. Now I've had to fetch 'em all back in again, and I nearly lost some newborns."

"Who are you talking about?"

"He calls himself Farmer Frederick and he writes that Farmer Frederick's Forecast every week in the *Ashfordly Gazette*, he's just been going a month or two. I reckon nowt to him, Nick, I don't think he's ever got a forecast right."

He went across to a magazine rack beside a Windsor chair near the fireplace and eased out this week's copy of the *Gazette*, turning to the page in question. Tucked into the bottom right-hand corner was a short piece bearing the title "Farmer Frederick's Forecast", followed by the worthy fellow's account of the weather which could be expected.

In this case, it said that because the weather during the first week in October last had been mild and dry with sunshine and clear skies, then the same could be expected in the first week of March this year.

"And was the first week in October like that?" I asked.

"Nay, Mr Rhea, how should I know? I don't keep them sort of records."

"Have you written to complain about the forecasts?" was my next question.

"Nay, I wouldn't do that. I mean, if it says so in the paper, you expect it to be right, don't you? I wondered if the paper had printed the wrong week's forecast or summat."

"Well, my suggestion is that you ignore Farmer Frederick. Listen to the radio or watch the television instead. Or better still, trust your own judgement."

But Jack wasn't the only farmer to complain. A week or two later, I was visiting Angus Stirling at his smallholding near Elsinby and he happened to comment as he checked his stock of pigs, "Yon Farmer Frederick's got it wrong again," he said. "He wrote that I had to sow my peas on the feast of St Chad, and I've lost 'em all and the other week he said that pale moonlight meant rain, and there wasn't a drop. Then he wrote summat about St Eulalie's Day being good for apples, that was in February, and, well, yon saint's French, nowt to do with Yorkshire farmers. Why would he mention a French saint?"

"Perhaps he has no idea that Eulalie is French," I suggested. "Now, this forecaster, is it Farmer Frederick from the *Ashfordly Gazette*?" I put to him.

"Who else? I dunno where they found that chap, but if there's one thing he can't do, it's forecast the weather."

In the weeks that followed, I discovered other forecasting disasters by the famous Frederick because I started to read his column, chiefly out of curiosity to discover just how often he was right or wrong. Almost invariably, he was wrong, although the law of averages did mean he was right from time to time. When April came, for example, he forecast showers, heavy at times, with bright intervals — that was inevitable in April, but in another case he added that *If the birch leaf is the size of a farthing on the Feast of Our Lady of Kazan, you will have corn in the barn.* He did not add that Our Lady of Kazan was a Russian version of the Blessed Virgin Mary — and that that forecast was for Russian, not Yorkshire, farmers.

I read another of Farmer Frederick's forecasts in which he stated, in April, that the weather on the night of the feast day of St Peter shows what weather we shall have during the forthcoming forty days. It was a version of the St Swithin's Day legend, but the snag was that there were several St Peters, all with different feast days. The best known was St Peter, the famous apostle who became the first pope, his feast day being shared with St Paul on June 29, but Farmer Frederick was writing about the weather in April. I consulted one of my dictionaries of saints' days — it confirmed that St Peter the Apostle's feast day was June 29, but St Peter Arbues has a feast day on September 17, St Peter Chrysologus has his on December 4, St Peter Exorcista's is held on December 9 with St Peter of Verona's feast day being on April 29. There is also a St Petronius who has a feast day on October 4 but I did not think that the weather on the feast day of St Peter of Verona, which is an Italian town, would have any bearing on the weather on Yorkshire farms, even if his feast day was in April. Somebody, Farmer Frederick in other words, had got his forecasting facts wrong.

It never occurred to me that Farmer Frederick was the pseudonym of Claude Jeremiah Greengrass until Claude arrived at Aidensfield police house one Wednesday morning around half past ten. There was a look of anger and anxiety on his face as I opened the door.

"Morning, Claude," I tried to appear cheerful. "To what do I owe this pleasure?"

"I've come to report a larceny," he announced.

"You'd better come in then," and I invited him into my office. Mary was brewing a coffee and when she noticed Claude's presence, she brought him one.

"Now this is what I call service." His face relaxed a little as he settled in the chair beside my desk. "You'd never get old Blaketon giving me coffee at Ashfordly nick."

"So, Claude," I asked. "A larceny, you said. What's been stolen?"

"A book."

"Yours?"

"Aye, of course. I can read you know."

"It's a funny thing to steal, Claude, was there a break-in at your house? Are we talking about a housebreaking or a burglary or something similar?"

"No, I'd left it in that telephone kiosk at the end of my lane, last night. By mistake. It was gone this morning. You can't trust anybody these days, can you?"

"What's the title?"

"*Weather Wisdom*; it's a hardback written by a chap called Walter Halliday in 1802."

"Maybe somebody's handed it in as found property?" I suggested. "It's hardly the sort of thing anybody would pinch. Nobody's handed it in to me, but I'll check with Ashfordly if you wait a moment."

I rang Ashfordly Police Station to request PC Alf Ventress to check the Found Property register, but the line was engaged. I took the opportunity to quiz Claude a little more as we sipped our coffees.

"So how did you come to leave that book in an isolated telephone kiosk?" I asked.

He blinked furiously across the top of his mug and squirmed in his seat.

"You fellers do operate a confidential service, don't you?" he asked quietly.

"Of course, Claude."

"Aye, well, I got that book a week or two back, from that second-hand book stall at the fair, you know. Full of information, it is, about the weather. So I rang the *Gazette* and offered my services, doing weather forecasts, from that book. Dead easy it is, you just turn up the right day and it's all there."

"Really, as easy as that, eh?"

"Aye, and did you know that a snowstorm in May is worth a wagon load of hay, or that when the wind's in the west, the weather's at its best?"

"All fascinating stuff, Claude, but you're no journalist! You're not a writer!"

"Aye, well, I didn't actually write the stuff." He was blinking even more furiously now. "The paper rings me, on a Tuesday night; I haven't a phone, so I go to that kiosk near my road end and they ring me there. I pick the right bit of weather from that book, and they take it all down. They call me Farmer Frederick, that's 'cos they think I'm a farmer. I get two guineas for every forecast, not bad money eh?"

"So you went to the kiosk last night to do your stuff, and forgot to take the book home?"

"Aye, and when I went back this morning, it had gone. It's important I get it back, Mr Rhea, I mean, how can I make my forecasts without that book, eh?"

"You could always hang a bit of seaweed outside or watch the smoke rising from the chimneys in Aidensfield," I laughed.

"That's all amateurish stuff, Mr Rhea," he grinned. "You're talking to a professional, you know, a published forecaster."

When the line was free, I rang Alf Ventress at Ashfordly Police Station. He checked his records but there was no record of the book being handed in. He said he would make a note, just in case anyone did return it later. The next problem was whether or not to record this as a crime.

After discussing it with Claude, I felt it best to regard it as Lost Property, the reasoning being that if the book had apparently been abandoned in a telephone kiosk, the taker could hardly be charged with stealing it. Claude was happy to know that if the book was found, it would be restored to him. "So what can I do about my forecasting?" he asked.

"Claude," I put to him, "you're a countryman, you probably know far more about the weather than is contained in that book. Use your own knowledge for the forecasts."

As the weeks went by, Farmer Frederick's forecasts did become more accurate and most definitely had more application to our locality or the moors in general. Claude's lost book never turned up, but no one else knew that Claude Jeremiah Greengrass was the Farmer Frederick, the famous and fabulous forecaster. Several weeks later, I asked how he obtained the information for his now fairly accurate forecasts.

"I listen to the farming programme on the radio," he said. "They do a weather forecast every week. Pretty accurate, they are, an' all."

And he blinked wickedly.

5. GREENGRASS ON THE HOOF

When the plunging hoofs were gone.
WALTER DE LA MARE, 1873–1956

My earlier *Constable* books recount some of the adventures, or perhaps the word should be misadventures, of Claude Jeremiah Greengrass when he tried to breed or deal with animals. Inevitably, things went wrong with Claude's enterprises but people like him never learn from their mistakes. Indeed, it was a typical Greengrass "mistake" that led to another of his doubtful cash-generating schemes. Even now, I am not sure whether he deliberately set out to trick gullible people, amongst whom I counted myself, or whether he did make a genuine error.

It began like this: land-owning people who lived upon the moors acted as keepers of seaside donkeys during the winter; after a hectic summer season of carrying fare-paying passengers along the beaches in a boring, never-ending trek, these tired, patient old mokes were sent away to good homes to recuperate. The seaside donkey owners paid a small fee to their temporary keepers, and country children loved to have these delightful animals living near their homes, if only during the late autumn and winter months. Donkeys are such lovely, patient creatures and there is no doubt they won the hearts of youngsters in Aidensfield.

Perhaps the keeper of the largest number of seaside donkeys was Claude Jeremiah Greengrass.

He had some rough pastureland on the edge of the moor, alongside some old but storm-proof buildings, and so he could accommodate about two dozen donkeys. The fees they generated provided a useful income for the scruffy old character and he did allow the village children to visit the donkeys, feed them and even ride them from time to time. Lots of village children spent hours looking after their new friends upon the Greengrass ranch. It is fair to add that Claude did look after them very well indeed, taking care over their feeding and stabling arrangements, and ensuring they were carefully groomed with due attention to their hooves. There is no doubt the donkeys were happy and contented with Greengrass.

I ought to add at this stage that there is a long-standing belief in both the North York Moors and elsewhere, that no one has seen a dead donkey. I have referred to this legend on previous occasions but it bears repeating — ask any of your friends or relations if they have ever seen a dead donkey, and the answer will almost certainly be "no". There will be exceptions of course, but while dead horses, cattle, dogs, cats, deer, foxes and rabbits are not at all unusual, a dead donkey is indeed a rarity. In fact, it is such a rarity that people would, at one time, travel long distances in the hope of seeing one, believing it brought good fortune to those who set their eyes upon it. In some parts of England, any person seeing a dead donkey had to leap three times over the carcass if they desired the very best of good fortune.

There is on record the case of a donkey's carcass being brought into a knacker's yard whereupon every employee leapt three times over the carcass in the firm belief that it would enable them to win the football pools.

The account does not state whether or not they did win any money, but the point remains that, even in modern times, the sight of a dead donkey is believed to be the herald of fortune.

It is not the only good-luck charm involving donkeys. There used to be a scheme known as "up goes the donkey" which was a stunt performed at many fairgrounds. Fairground entertainers would shout to the crowds that as soon as enough money had been gathered, the donkey which was fastened to the foot of a tall pole or a long ladder, would be made to ascend the pole or ladder and balance on the top. Always, two more pennies were required — there was never quite enough money to persuade the donkey to perform that trick. Those who witnessed the sight of the balancing donkey would be blessed with everlasting good fortune — the snag was that no one ever saw it happen.

Knowing of all these quaint beliefs and customs, I discovered, quite by chance, that one of the donkeys cared for by Claude Jeremiah Greengrass was quite aged. Paler in colour than his companions, he was a lovely old stallion called Rodney and he was spared the rigours of entertaining children who came to the Greengrass ranch. He could be fed with carrots and he could be fussed over and groomed by caring youngsters, but he was not for riding. He was far too old for that, Claude insisted.

Claude showed Rodney to me during one of my periodic visits and explained that the old chap really was getting too old for the rigours of seaside rides.

"Poor old Rodney should be put out to grass," Claude suggested.

"You'll see to that?" I put to him.

"It's up to his owner, not me," Claude said, before adding. "It wouldn't surprise me if poor old Rodney called it a day very soon. He spends a lot of time asleep; I think his days are numbered. I've had the vet out to see him; he says it's just old age and reckons Rodney will just fade away. He thinks it won't be long before he goes to that happy grazing ground in the sky."

Then the unthinkable actually happened: Rodney died. His end came while there was a traction engine rally in Aidensfield. As the crowds were milling around a field which adjoined Claude's property, Rodney fell asleep in one of Claude's spacious outbuildings. He passed away very peacefully on a bed of dry hay. The important thing from Claude's point of view was that the carcass now reclined on his premises.

Knowing the legend of the dead donkey, and the good fortune such a sight would bring to those who witnessed it, Claude did not intend to miss the opportunity presented to him. It was especially timely because there was a ready-made audience in the adjoining field. Acting with commendable speed, he erected a sign on the gate between his premises and the traction engine rally. In bold lettering, it announced, *Dead Donkey. A rare sight that brings good luck. Entrance 2s.6d. First party of visitors — 4 p.m.*

He then went around ringing a big brass hand-bell to draw attention to his offer and sure enough, a queue began to form at the gate.

"Passed away in his sleep during the night, he did," Claude was telling his customers. "Poor old chap. Rodney was his name, a lovely animal, gentle with the kids . . . he loved kids, he really did. And now he's gone. He didn't suffer. There'll never be another chance to see him. This is a once-in-a-lifetime chance to see a dead donkey. Good luck is waiting for you just round the corner, folks."

I discovered this latest Greengrass enterprise as the patient queue numbered about fifteen. It was a few minutes to four and Claude was standing at the gate ringing his bell and shouting that the dead donkey tour was about to commence. The next opportunity to see a dead donkey would be in an hour's time.

"Are you joining us, Mr Rhea?" Claude asked, with a mischievous glint in his eye. "You could do with a bit of luck, I'll bet."

On impulse, I decided I should see this incredible sight. After all, it might never happen again during my lifetime, so I paid my half-crown to Claude. He said I would never regret the investment. Then, after checking his watch, he announced it was time for the first party to depart. He altered his notice to say the next tour would be at 5 p.m., and off we set with Claude leading the way.

Outside a decrepit old shed, he paused. "In here," he whispered to the tourists. "Now, I've got some hens sitting in this shed: upstairs they are, and I don't want 'em disturbed. A dozen or more birds on a dozen or more clutches, there'll be a few good chicks to come out of that lot, so just follow me quietly. And be respectful in the presence of death, if you don't mind."

A deferential silence enveloped the party as Claude opened the battered wooden doors and led us inside. The interior was gloomy, there being no windows but the floor was covered with hay and straw and there was a cosy warmth within. It felt very snug and dry. Along the rear wall was a number of stalls, each separated from the next by a tall wooden partition known in the North York Moors as a skel-beast. Around the walls was a type of gallery which formed the first-floor landing perhaps six or eight feet wide. It was supported upon wooden poles which stood upon the floor, their bases lost among deep hay and straw. Access was via a ladder and I could see that a thick carpet of hay covered most of that landing floor.

"My hens are up there," Claude whispered to us. "Sitting well, they are. Good dockers are hard to come by . . . Now, follow me, and keep quiet . . ."

He was edging around the interior of the wall, treading lightly and carefully in the hay as he led us in single file to the rear stalls. Exercising great care to avoid alarming Claude's nesting hens, I could see that the man ahead of me was having a problem. At first, I was unsure of the cause of his distress, but he had pulled a handkerchief from his pocket and was wiping his watering eyes while endeavouring to stifle a severe fit of sneezing.

"Are you all right?" I manoeuvred myself alongside and whispered my concern.

"I'm allergic to hay dust," he sniffed. "I didn't realise it would be so thick in here. I thought the floor would be covered with straw, not hay. There's a lot of hay here."

"Hush, all of you!" hissed Claude. "I don't want my hens upset, they're at a critical stage of brooding . . ."

"Sorry," said the man.

"Shall I lead you out?" I asked the fellow.

"It's a bit late now," he sniffed. "It's as far to go out as it is to go in, besides, I really do want to see that dead donkey! I've never seen one, you know. I can't give up now."

Then we approached the corner stall. In the gloom, I could see that a large green tarpaulin sheet covered something very bulky which was lying among the hay.

"Gather round, everyone," whispered Claude in sepulchral tones. It was almost like a graveside gathering, I thought. It wouldn't have surprised me if Claude had muttered a prayer for the dead and then, just as he was about to remove the tarpaulin to reveal the hallowed carcass of the dead Rodney, my companion with the allergy produced a mighty sneeze. In volume, it sounded like an exploding bomb inside an echo chamber, and he repeated the clamour in a non-stop, rapidly produced series of thunderous bellows. Suddenly, the entire barn was filled with sounds like thunderclaps as the poor fellow began to sneeze himself silly. As the echo of his sneezing filled the void in which we all stood and reverberated about the rafters, the unhappy hens upstairs became extremely alarmed. Each one blasted from its nest with a cackling and a squawking that would raise the dead. The terrified birds now squawked and flapped flew around the barn, first alarmed by the noise and then terrified by the influx of people below them while the originator of their distress continued to sneeze as if he was blasting stubborn stone from a remote quarry.

Claude's solemn moment had evaporated because everyone else, including myself, burst out laughing. This increased the weird noises within the confined space — and then the tarpaulin began to move.

As the hens cackled and flapped in their panic, and the man continued to produce his salvos, the tarpaulin slid to the ground to reveal a very alive Rodney who was standing firm and square on all four hooves. The old donkey, apparently restored to life by the bedlam around him, issued his own triumphant bellow of "hee-haw, hee-haw" as someone shouted. "Claude, you old twister! He's not dead . . . that donkey was just asleep. He's just woken up . . ."

"No, honest, no, I thought he was a goner, honest I did. I mean, there was no breathing . . ."

Everyone began to boo Claude. Among the chaos, the sneezer continued his barrage of noise as he ran for the door and opened it to gain some relief. Out flew the hens, still cackling and squawking as they emerged into the daylight.

"It's money-back time, Claude," I whispered to him. "You nearly got away with it that time . . . dead donkeys, my foot!"

"But, but . . . look, Constable, I thought he was dead. Honest, I did. I mean, I covered him up, decent-like, when I found him and he never moved, not even a twitch of his ears."

"Claude!" I held out my hand for the half-crowns. "Refunds if you don't mind! And suppose we donate all your takings to a home for sick donkeys?"

"A good idea, Constable. And shame on you, Claude Greengrass!" snapped a little woman. "Taking advantage of poor widows like me!"

"I thought he was dead, I did, I really did," pleaded Claude and he blinked sheepishly. Then he began to hand over the money.

"Well, he didn't bring you much luck, did he?" chuckled one of the men.

And as Rodney trotted towards the open door, he hee-hawed all the more as he smelt the fresh breeze of a splendid day. His call of triumph was matched by an almighty and probably final sneeze from the suffering allergic gentleman as he savoured the beautiful fresh moorland air.

"Where's all my hens gone?" asked Claude as he emerged from the barn.

"I think they've gone to look at the traction engines," chuckled one of the men. "Or mebbe it's donkey engines they want to see? They'd make quieter nesting sites!"

* * *

I am old enough to recall pig-killing days in rural areas. Almost every cottager kept at least one pig, and often more. My grandfather kept lots on his farm and my own father kept a couple of large whites in pigsties within our cottage grounds. In some cases the pigs were used for breeding and the resultant piglets were fattened and sold to butchers, dealers or bacon-curing warehouses. In others, country people, like my father, killed their own pigs on the premises — Dad was a qualified butcher. On all the farms, smallholdings and cottage premises on the moors, pig-killing day was one of excitement and anticipation.

The neighbours offered assistance and children were recruited to help with the killing, the salting, the scraping of the skin with scrapers like upturned candlesticks and sundry other tasks. The ladies worked in the kitchen rendering the fat which came from the unfortunate animal. This became lard, and the surplus pieces of chunky fat left over from lard making, were fried, salted and eaten as a delicacy known as scrappings. It was a well-known saying that everything from a pig is used, except the squeak. Inevitably, on pig-killing days, there was a surplus of meat and other pieces, so these were distributed around the village free of charge. This was known as pig cheer.

Later, salted hams would be seen hanging from the rafters as they were allowed to cure in the dry atmosphere of the house. Fresh bacon was eaten with gusto and there were trotters and other mysterious bits which were used for making brawn, intestines for making sausage skins, blood for black puddings and even the bladder was utilised as a football by the boys. The best time for killing the family pig was when there was an "r" in the month, especially in winter with November and December being the favourites. Pigs salted without there being an "r" in the month would not "take salt", i.e. the flesh would not cure, it was said. It was often considered wise to avoid killing pigs when the moon was on the wane. There is a moorland verse which reads

Allus kill a pig when the moon is waxing,
Never kill a pig when the moon is a-waning.

If a pig was killed when the moon was waning, it was thought the flesh would go rotten. Many families had their own recipe for curing the bacon and hams.

Although I was brought up in a society where pig-killing days were normal, I must confess I disliked my involvement. In fact, it put me off eating meat for many years. Looking back upon those days, I don't think the pigs suffered and there was immense care to avoid any form of cruelty. Indeed, many pig owners had become attached to their solitary animal, but the needs of the family had to take precedence over any emotion. A pig, lovable though it might be, was a form of security for a rural family. It was there to be used as a means of keeping the family well fed, but for a little lad watching a pig being stunned with a captive bolt humane killer and then being bled through a massive gash in its throat among all the paraphernalia of a pig-killing day, it was not a pleasant experience.

I believe there was a period, sometime after 1927, when it became unlawful for cottagers to kill their own pigs on private premises, the idea being that the animals had to be sent to a licensed slaughter man who operated in a properly equipped slaughterhouse. It was this kind of progress which, although upsetting the cottagers because it changed a long-standing way of rural life, eventually led to the decline of pigs being kept in cottage gardens. Inevitably, some rural folks did continue to keep pigs and to kill them privately in defiance of the regulations. One such person was Claude Jeremiah Greengrass.

I suspect that he had decided to kill his own pig rather than transport it to Ashfordly Slaughterhouse to avoid spending money. Claude, being a countryman of long experience, would know how to kill a pig in the traditional manner. I understand that he had the necessary equipment in and around his home, including a creel and a scalding tub, and most certainly he would have access to a humane killer. As the preparations for killing a pig are underway, it is questionable whether the animal is aware of what is happening. Pigs are highly intelligent and it is fair to say that Claude's large white sow, inexplicably called Miss Nixon, seemed to sense that all was not well on that Monday in November.

While Claude was going about the business of preparation, he had left the sneck off the door of Miss Nixon's sty. Miss Nixon, sensing the door was open rather wider than usual, poked her snout towards the opening whereupon the door swung wide. Miss Nixon lost no time in leaving the confines of her sty and, grunting with joy, decided to go for a walk. Claude, busy with his equipment and anxious to complete the unpleasant task as quickly as possible, did not notice her absence for some time. In that time, some ten or fifteen minutes, Miss Nixon had found her way from Claude's ranch and on to the open moor which surrounded his cottage. Bristling with sheer pleasure, the happy pig began to root among the heather, savouring the juicy roots of plants she had never tasted. It is fair to say that Miss Nixon was, for the time being, a very contented sow. It could be argued that she had no idea of her fate because she did not stray very far from Claude's ranch, nor did she attempt to run away or hide.

It was while on patrol and descending a quiet moorland road into Aidensfield, that I noticed the uncommon sight of a large white pig, a robust sow by the look of it, rooting unsupervised among the heather. As it was very close to the Greengrass abode, I reckoned it could only have come from there and so I drove into the grounds, parked my minivan and began to search for Claude. I called his name and found him as I appeared around a corner of a building; he looked flustered and began blinking rapidly when he saw me, knowing that I had recognised the equipment in his yard as that which was necessary to kill and cure a pig. He was working among it as I approached him.

"Just checking my equipment, Mr Rhea, in case I want to sell it," he blinked even more furiously as he made his excuses. "Summat up, is there, you being here?" Until that point, I had no idea that he was preparing to kill Miss Nixon. Now I realised what he was hoping to do, but breaches of those regulations were not really a matter for the police.

"Have you a large white pig?" I asked.

"Who wants to know?" I sensed his caution now. "It's not the ministry, is it?"

"No, it's me. I want to know." I realised he was being devious now; his eyes were blinking faster than the shutter of a high-speed camera.

"Why do you want to know?" His caution was still there.

"Because there's one out there, on the moor," I said, waving my hand in the general direction of the free-range pig. "A large white, a sow by the look of it."

At that news, he rushed off to examine the sty and, upon seeing the door standing open, realised that Miss Nixon had escaped. "She's got away, Mr Rhea. My best sow! Come on Alfred," he shouted for his dog. "And you, Constable, can you help me round her up? I want her back in my yard before she gets any big ideas of freedom into her head."

And so it was that I found myself trudging through the thick, damp heather of the moors armed with a long stick. The idea was very simple — we had to manoeuvre ourselves into position behind Miss Nixon and drive her towards Claude's yard, the gate of which he had left open to receive her. Alfred, the lurcher, was to assist us. The snag was that lurchers are not very good at emulating sheepdogs; that idea was further complicated because pigs do not behave like sheep. They do not like being driven anywhere if they can avoid it, and the moment we appeared behind Miss Nixon with our vicious-looking sticks, she spotted us. Snorting and squealing in protest, she began to trot rapidly in the wrong direction. She was heading away from Claude's smallholding.

"Alfred, turn her, fetch her back!" snapped Claude, but Alfred merely barked and started to chase Miss Nixon. Claude shouted, "Heel, Alfred, you daft bugger! You've frightened her . . . leave off!"

But Alfred was enjoying the chase. It wasn't often that creatures larger than him ran away from him and he sensed that, on this occasion, he possessed some awesome power — which he was going to use. As the sow's pace increased from a trot to a gallop, so Alfred maintained his position close to her heels.

He urged her forward by snapping and biting at her hind legs as Miss Nixon endeavoured to avoid him. She did manage to lash out with her hind feet and, perhaps fortunately for Alfred, failed to make contact. In spite of that, she was moving very fast — and a fast-moving pig is a formidable object, not the easiest of creatures to bring to a halt. Unlike horses or dogs, there is not a lot for a catcher to seize, such as thick fur or a leather halter or collar. Alfred was certainly incapable of halting the pig; in fact, his yapping and nipping was encouraging the sow to greater efforts as she increased the distance between herself and her sty. It wasn't long, therefore, before dog and pig had left me and Claude a long way behind. We could merely shout and watch as Miss Nixon, with teats swaying, headed into the centre of Aidensfield with Alfred still snapping and yapping at her heels. The chase was most definitely on and we had no idea where it was going to end.

The problem facing Claude and me was how to get ahead of the galloping sow. Somehow, we had to get in front of her to steer her into a confined space — a shed, barn or paddock would be ideal. We needed something to contain her, if only temporarily. Even a large field would be better than the open road. If only there was a gate open *en route*, it might be possible to beg a lift on a passing vehicle for one of us to get ahead and steer her into some secure place. But there were no open gates as Miss Nixon, with Alfred behind her, was surging ever forward in her gallant bid for freedom.

As she entered the main street a long way ahead of me and Claude, albeit with Alfred in extremely close attendance, Arnold Merryweather's lumbering old bus chanced to appear from the opposite direction. I saw Miss Nixon momentarily slow her gallop at the appearance of the bus some distance ahead, but then she realised it was not heading for her. Satisfied that it was not a threat, she resumed her former pace. But as she hurtled towards the centre of Aidensfield, Arnold's groaning old bus pulled up at the official stop to disgorge some passengers.

By this time, Miss Nixon was rapidly approaching that same bus stop, albeit without any intention of catching the bus. When eight or nine ladies and gentlemen of varying ages and sizes, one with a poodle on a lead and two with pushchairs, emerged from the bus, I believe that Miss Nixon thought they had been recruited to thwart her dash for freedom. She decided to avoid them. And, by a stroke of good fortune (for her), there was a convenient opening in which she could seek sanctuary.

It was the door of the Aidensfield Stores and it was standing open as it always did, winter and summer alike.

Just inside, on the floor, was one of Joe Steel's carefully constructed pieces of artwork, a six-foot high pyramid comprising tins of beans, soup and fruit in syrup, and beyond that, a row of tin buckets, yard brushes and shovels, the latter leaning against the shelves upon the wall and the handles of the yard brushes leaning against the contents of the shelves. Those shelves contained many other provisions, ranging from jars of sweets to bottles of cough syrup; there were even items of crockery for sale such as cups, saucers, plates and mugs.

Joe, realising that there would be an influx of people from the bus, had retreated from building his pyramid of tins and he was safe behind the counter, ready to relieve them of their cash. He was practising his smile when Miss Nixon, hotly pursued by Alfred, barged into the shop like a bull elephant at the climax of a death-defying charge. Her first contact was the pyramid of tins. They flew in all directions with a clanging tone, the pig standing on some and losing her balance before rolling her huge body into the buckets and brooms which were next in line.

As the brushes were swept before the advancing Miss Nixon, the tips of their tall handles, in one brilliantly executed movement, cleared all the shelves of provisions and crockery. The whole of Joe's carefully crafted display crashed to the floor with salvos of noise, the sound of breaking crockery being noticeable even to those of us outside. By now, Claude and I, both of us breathless after the chase, had arrived outside the shop, as had the passengers from Arnold Merryweather's bus. None dared to enter as the terrified Miss Nixon, with Alfred still in hot pursuit, stampeded around Joe Steel's shop.

Joe was shouting at the pig, the pig was squealing with terror, Alfred was barking with uncontrolled excitement and all these sounds were accompanied by the noise of falling tins and crashing crockery. Then suddenly, Miss Nixon halted her gallop. She had found the fruit and vegetables. Ignoring the yapping Alfred at her heels, she began to tuck into Joe's display of tomatoes, peaches and soft fruit, guzzling with undisguised enjoyment as the rest of us arrived to assess the situation. Now that Miss Nixon had ended her race, Alfred very quickly became bored. He sniffed at some of the provisions on the shop floor, rejected them as not tasty enough for a dog, and trotted out to greet his master. Claude was entering the shop with me in close attendance, both of us panting with the exertions of the morning.

"Greengrass, you'll pay for this!" Joe was normally a placid, gentle sort of man but the chaos in his shop had caused even him to lose a little of his composure. "Get that animal out of here . . ."

"She'll have to stay till I get a line on her leg," puffed Claude.

"I don't want her galloping all over t'village again. Now we've cornered her, we'll have to keep her. So shut all the doors and keep her in . . . I need a bit of rope . . ."

"I'll sell you a clothes line!" snapped Joe. "Cash!"

As Miss Nixon snuffled and grunted with satisfaction among the fruit and vegetables, Claude bought a clothes line. With Miss Nixon concentrating upon the free food, Claude had no difficulty tying one end to her right hind leg. She raised absolutely no objection to this and continued to guzzle with noisy enjoyment as the shop slowly filled with people from Arnold's bus. They stepped over the debris and made for the counter as Joe was saying, "Claude, you'll have to pay for this damage . . . look at my crockery, my vegetables . . ."

"Aye, well, it wasn't intended, Joe. She got away on us, Mr Rhea'll confirm that . . . I mean, we never chased her in here, she just turned in. I reckon she's an outlaw, Joe," and Claude chuckled at his modest joke.

"No excuses, Claude. I'll tot up the damage and send you a bill. Now, get that animal out so I can get my shop straight."

"What's going to happen to the pig?" asked one lady.

"She's going for t'chop," said Claude. "It's pig-killing time. I think she knew, that's why she ran for it."

"You're not going to kill that lovely animal, Mr Greengrass?" twittered Mrs Arkwright, another lady from the bus. "Surely not, especially after she's made such a spirited bid for freedom!"

"Aye, well, us country folks can't be sentimental about animals; this pig's part of my income, you see, and pig-killing days mean money . . ."

"I'll buy her off you!" decided Mrs Arkwright. "My son keeps pigs and sheep and things, for breeding, not for slaughtering. Now, I'll give you a good price, full market value, in cash, immediately Mr Greengrass. I do not want that animal to be slaughtered, she's such a delightfully spirited creature!"

Claude blinked at the assembled gathering and looked at me for guidance.

"It seems a good bargain to me, Claude," was all I could say.

Mrs Arkwright was prepared to pay £32 10s. for Miss Nixon and in seconds had her purse open and the cash in her hand. But she smiled as she handed it to Joe Steel.

"I think Mr Steel might want some compensation out of this," she said sweetly to Claude.

"But it's my money, my pig money!" protested Claude, but Joe simply beamed in return.

"I'll work out what the cost of the damage is, Claude, and let you have the change, if there is any. But remember you do owe me for that sack of potatoes you bought last week, and there's your newspaper bill and I seem to remember you got some tins of beans and peaches the other day, before that pig of yours got at them . . . now, if you'd kindly move that animal away from my vegetable rack, I'll get this place back to normal."

"Aye, well, it's not my pig anymore," beamed Claude. "It's hers."

"My son will be outside with the pickup," smiled Mrs Arkwright. "He always comes to meet me off the bus. I'll get him to remove Claudia."

"Claudia? Her name's Miss Nixon," spluttered Claude.

"Not anymore," chuckled Mrs Arkwright. "I think Claudia is such a lovely name for a sow. She'll remind me of you, Claude."

Ten minutes later, the well-fed and now docile Claudia was persuaded to climb up a ramp into the rear of Alan Arkwright's pickup and, to the cheers of the assembled crowd, the happy sow was transported away to a new life. Alfred barked his farewell. Now, I had to walk back to the Greengrass ranch to collect my minivan and Claude accompanied me.

"I've got nowt out of all that, Constable, nowt but a load of trouble. And I haven't even got a pig to kill!"

"You weren't going to kill Miss Nixon, were you?" I asked.

He blinked furiously and said, "Aye, well, not exactly, but a feller has to earn a living somehow, Mr Rhea, and pigs is good money earners."

"Especially if you sell them alive," I smiled.

Then he halted in his tracks.

"She's taken that new clothes line of mine, has that woman!" he cried. "Now, there's a rotten thing to do . . ."

"You don't need it for another pig? You're not thinking of buying another pig, Claude?" I laughed.

"I am not, I've had enough of pigs for one day. Mind, I was looking forward to a bacon breakfast tomorrow morning. I reckon I'll have to make do with porridge instead."

And Alfred barked. He liked his own bit of pig cheer after a pig-killing day, but would have to make do with Claude's leftovers on this occasion.

* * *

On another occasion, Claude Jeremiah Greengrass decided to take half a dozen ewes to Ashfordly Cattle Mart. The animals would be entered for sale that Friday and Claude hoped his sturdy animals would attract a buyer. At that time, sheep were commanding good prices, with black-faced moorland ewes being particularly sought after. Claude was confident of a profitable visit to mart.

The snag was that he had no vehicle in which to carry the sheep. His pickup truck was open at the back which meant that the silly ewes would surely leap out because he had no means of securing them, such as a net or a removable hard cover. He could not afford a larger enclosed van or a cattle truck although he did possess a small motor car. It was a Ford Anglia of doubtful vintage and uncertain reliability; he used it from time to time when he wished to carry human passengers, as opposed to his pickup which he regarded as business transport. The pickup usually carried inactive commodities like logs or bags of potatoes, although Alfred, his lurcher, could be relied upon not to leap out when the vehicle was in progress.

Faced with an urgent need to transport his ewes to market, Claude decided to pack them into his Ford Anglia. Living sheep are not noted for their intelligence and it is fair to say that Claude had some difficulty persuading six of them to climb into the rear seat, and into the front passenger seat, of his Ford Anglia. Claude did not consider using the car boot because it was full of antique furniture which he hoped to sell at some future stage. His use of the phrase "antique furniture" was a euphemism for rubbishy old junk.

Happily, black-faced ewes do have horns which serve as handles on occasions and these animals were also particularly well endowed with heavy wool, thus making it comparatively easy for the powerful Claude to seize each animal, manhandle it into a suitable position and then thrust it into the car before slamming the door to enclose it. After a period of some effort, during which he was encouraged by Alfred's barking, he had all six ewes safely inside the car. I do not know of any official record for the number of ewes that can be squeezed into a Ford Anglia, but it is fair to say that his car was quite full of wool.

One of the ewes, however, had managed to find its way on to the driving seat. This added to the problem of where Alfred was going to be carried — Claude could probably nurse Alfred, but it was doubtful whether he could nurse both Alfred and a fully grown sheep. He solved the problem by shouting at the animal as he clambered in beside it, then heaving the sheep across to the passenger side where another one already sat in bewilderment. Claude did manage to gain most of the driver's seat, whereupon he called Alfred who leapt on to his knee.

There is no doubt that Claude had difficulty seeing the road ahead due to Alfred's size and position, and furthermore he had trouble locating and operating the controls, particularly the gear lever and the steering wheel. The position and protesting movements of the two ewes which occupied the front passenger seat didn't help either. Regardless of the risks, Claude set off to drive to Ashfordly Mart; his car had assumed the appearance of a living sheepskin rug on wheels.

Unfortunately, he did not get very far. As he was struggling to guide his car down Slape Stone Bank, it transpired that Sergeant Blaketon was motoring up the self-same bank *en route* to pay me an official visit. Later, Blaketon described to me what then happened; he did so in the form of a written statement because he had witnessed a traffic accident.

He wrote:

I could not believe my eyes. Heading towards me down Slape Stone Bank on the outskirts of Aidensfield was a scruffy car which appeared to be driven by a dog. My first thought was that the car had been parked and the driver had left it without setting the handbrake, and that it had run away down the slope. The dog was in the driving seat and the car was full of sheep. There were sheep in the front passenger seat, another sitting between the two front seats and a further accumulation of sheep upon the rear seat. There appeared to be no human being in control of the vehicle because it was weaving about the road as if the steering was faulty, and so I drove on to the verge to avoid a collision. As it approached the point where I waited, the car swerved violently to its left and ran off the road, on to the open moor. It continued a few yards across the moor until it came to a steep-sided ditch; it ran into the ditch and overturned. I ran to the scene and found that there was a driver. It was Claude Jeremiah Greengrass and when I arrived, he was wedged into the driving seat of the overturned car by the weight of several sheep and one dog. I managed to lift out the dog, known as Alfred, and then dragged out Claude Jeremiah Greengrass, leaving all the sheep inside. One of them had a cut to the head, I noted, but it was a minor injury and no veterinary treatment was required. I was able to tip the car back on to its wheels because it was very finely balanced. As it was safe to leave the sheep in the car, I conveyed Mr Greengrass and his dog to his home at Aidensfield. Because a sheep was injured in the incident, it is reportable as a road traffic accident. I therefore made an official record of the event. The car and the sheep were later recovered from the scene and returned to the home of Mr Greengrass, the car being slightly damaged on the nearside where it had come to rest. None of the other sheep was hurt. When I asked Mr Greengrass why the car was full of sheep and a dog, he said, "I was going to take them all for a walk on the moor. Them sheep are pets, you know."

Sergeant Blaketon's verbal account of the incident was slightly more colourful than his official version, suggesting that Greengrass was a lunatic and that such an idiot had no right to be on the road in charge of a motor vehicle.

"So, Rhea," he said, when he had completed his written and verbal account for my benefit, "I suggest we prosecute Greengrass for careless driving!"

"I thought you said the dog was driving, Sergeant?" I joked.

"That sort of facetiousness is not funny, Rhea!" he grunted. "The fellow was driving carelessly at the least, I'd even say he was driving dangerously."

"He could put forward the defence of automatism," I said seriously.

"And what justification would he have for that, Rhea?"

"Well, if a motorist is stung by a wasp and swerves off the road as a result, it is possible to plead that it was an involuntary action, the result of the unexpected presence of the wasp. I would imagine that Claude might plead similarly — that the dog or the sheep had suddenly leapt on to his lap to obscure his view and prevent him having full control of the car. Automatism for one is automatism for another, Sergeant."

"He shouldn't have had the animals in his car, Rhea! A driver is always supposed to be in such a position that he or she has proper control of the vehicle, and furthermore, the load should be distributed or packed so that it does not cause danger to any other user of the road. And the number of passengers, or the manner in which they are carried, must not be likely to cause danger. I'm not sure whether a court would regard those sheep as a load or as passengers, but they were certainly not packed in a way that was suitable. I recommend prosecution, Rhea — for careless driving, failing to have proper control of a motor vehicle, driving with a dangerous load and being a driver who was not in a position to have proper control of his vehicle. Now, have you checked Greengrass's insurance?"

I had, and it appeared to be valid and in order but a closer examination of his certificate of insurance said he could use his Ford Anglia only for social, domestic and pleasure purposes. In that car, he was not covered for business purposes.

"I think he was taking those animals to Ashfordly Mart, Rhea, it was market day and he was heading that way. That means he was using his car for business."

"But you'll never prove it, Sergeant. In his statement to you, he said he was taking them all for a walk on the moor. I mean, that's not business, that's pleasure."

"If you believe that, Rhea, you're dafter than I thought! Taking sheep for a walk!"

"It's not what I believe that counts, Sergeant, it's what we can prove before a court of law. And there is no proof Claude was using the car for business purposes."

"The fact that it was full of sheep is enough, I'd say," Blaketon was adamant. "Submit a report to that effect. Book him for not having his car insured for the carriage of livestock for business purposes."

And so I had to book Claude Jeremiah for several motoring offences which arose from that incident and Sergeant Blaketon recommended prosecution. But after due consideration of the file, the superintendent declined to prosecute.

He said there was no evidence that Claude was using the car for business purposes — taking dogs and even pet sheep for walks on the moor was a domestic occurrence — and Sergeant Blaketon had not proved that Claude was driving at the time he saw the car on the road. According to Sergeant Blaketon's statement, a dog was driving the car on the road and dogs could not be prosecuted. At the time Blaketon saw Greengrass in the driving seat, the car was off the road and thus no offence was committed.

"I'll get that man before I retire, so help me!" vowed Sergeant Blaketon.

6. GREENGRASS ON TOUR

> Our deeds still travel with us . . .
> GEORGE ELIOT, 1819–80

When Claude Jeremiah Greengrass teamed up with Arnold Merryweather to run coach trips in one or other of Arnold's pair of old buses, I must admit I experienced a fluttering of apprehension. I could envisage countless breaches of traffic law, to say nothing of danger to the public and problems with offences against the regulations governing drivers, conductors and passengers. I couldn't imagine a level-headed businessman like Arnold accepting help or advice from Claude, even though there had been rumours of Claude's admiration for Hannah Pybus. She was the giant conductress who ensured Arnold's buses ran on time and made a profit.

Hannah, a spinster of the parish of Thackerston, was a most unattractive woman in her middle fifties. With hips so immense that she had to walk sideways down the aisles of a standard coach, she was well over six feet tall and was built like a gasometer. She walked with a sailor-like motion while her loose-fitting clothes concealed any semblance of a female shape. She had a freckled face with pale-brown eyes and a mop of sandy or rust-coloured hair held in place with tortoiseshell slides with a heavy red ribbon at the back.

Upon the death of her father, a successful sheep farmer, Hannah had required something to occupy her because, hitherto, she had spent her life caring for her old dad and helping him run the farm. Now that the farm, the equipment and all the livestock had been sold to provide her with a modest income, Hannah had moved into a small cottage but she was in need of an interest rather than a salary. When Arnold had advertised for a conductress on his service bus, she had seen it as a golden opportunity for travel and had applied for the job. Under her stern care, every passenger paid promptly, there was no trouble from boisterous children and Arnold's old coaches were regularly cleaned and serviced. It was evident that Hannah was good for Arnold Merryweather's business and that he had prospered due to her presence. It was that kind of success that prompted Arnold to think of expanding his enterprise, and so he bought another coach, a rather smart second-hand vehicle, thus bringing his fleet to three.

Having spent his capital on the additional coach, Arnold had to ensure that it was kept busy enough to earn its keep. Already, he ran a service bus around the villages in the Ashfordly-Aidensfield district, while his second coach was for hire on special occasions. Football-club outings, Women's Institute functions, trips to Scarborough or to Blackpool to see the lights or to York to the theatre or a pantomime were the sort of work that kept his second bus on the road. Arnold usually drove that one, leaving the service runs to an employed driver, supervised by Hannah.

With a third coach to maintain and keep busy, Arnold was open to ideas and, only a couple of days after Arnold's purchase graced his garage forecourt, it was Claude Jeremiah Greengrass who suggested he could be useful — he could drive the new bus on a mystery tour.

"Where to?" asked Arnold.

"How should I know?" blustered Claude. "It's a mystery tour, isn't it?"

"Yes, it's a mystery to the passengers, not to the driver! He has to know where he's going. You have to plan a route, Claude, with somewhere to stop for refreshments and toilets, and some object in mind like a stately home to visit or a zoo or the seaside or something entertaining. You've got to keep your passengers interested and occupied during the trip while not staying away too long, it hasn't to become a marathon. Half a day's about right, especially when pensioners are on board."

"You can't create much of a mystery in half a day," grumbled Claude.

"You can for folks who don't get out a lot; they're happy just to ride around looking at the moors or the sea and stopping at a nice café. So if you can come up with a suitable outing, I'll consider it."

"If I do come up with an idea, what's in it for me?" was Claude's next question.

"Well, I could share the profits on the day's outing, fifty-fifty after expenses have been met. I've got to allow for fuel, a driver's wages and so on, with a bit put by for the bus. A share always goes to the bus."

"Right, you're on!" beamed Claude. "A fifty-fifty profit-sharing job, then. Now, here's the good news. I can save you a driver's wages because I can drive the bus. I drove heavies in the army, you know, and military coaches. I have a licence."

"You have?" This was news to Arnold. He was often on the lookout for qualified PSV drivers for work at short notice, and this offered some relief for him. He went on. "Right, well, I think we might do business, Claude. You find a route for a mystery tour, then come back to me and we'll see about arranging something. And we can share the profits, eh? After deductions for expenses, of course."

I learned of this conversation from Arnold and advised him to check Claude's driving licence before allowing him to take control of a busload of passengers but it seemed that everything was in order. Claude returned a couple of days later with a plan which Arnold found acceptable. Arnold told me about it.

"He's caught me by surprise," Arnold laughed with good humour. "I've not even had time to put my own livery on the new bus. Mind you, it's very smart and a good polish up'll do the trick. I reckon I can manage without having to repaint it, especially if I've got work for it as soon as this!"

Arnold then explained that Claude had discovered that the Beatles were in concert at the Futurist Theatre in Scarborough. There was a huge interest in this new pop group from Liverpool and youngsters would queue all night in the hope of obtaining a ticket. According to Claude, he had learned from a confidential but highly reliable source that the famous four would be rehearsing at the theatre during the afternoon before their sell-out performance. He felt that his passengers might like to savour the atmosphere and even catch sight of the famous Beatles. His proposal was that he convey his mystified passengers to Scarborough and drop them outside the theatre, telling them to wait and watch because they would see the arrival of the Beatles at 2.30 p.m.

There were plenty of cafés and loos in the town and as the idea sounded fine, Arnold agreed to it and said he would advertise in Ashfordly rather than Aidensfield because of the likelihood of greater numbers of applicants for seats on the bus. The trip was arranged for a Thursday, leaving Ashfordly at 11 a.m., making a tour of the moors with a halt at Strensford for a fish-and-chip lunch, then on to Scarborough where Claude would park his bus outside the Futurist Theatre. His passengers would be told, at the last minute, that if they disembarked and stood near the stage door, they would see the Beatles. They should be back in Ashfordly by 4 p.m. or thereabouts.

And Claude guaranteed that they would see the Beatles — such was the reliability of his informant. Even without this inside knowledge, the trip was fully subscribed in advance, as these mystery tours always were and so, at the appointed time, Claude went to collect his passengers. They were all strangers to him, being Ashfordly folk. I chanced to be on duty that morning in Ashfordly marketplace as Claude arrived at the wheel of Arnold's bus. I watched him park the gleaming two-tone blue coach and saw him beaming with pride and amusement as his passengers, mainly pensioners, clambered on board. Among them was a lady I knew slightly — she was Mrs Alice Brown, the widowed mother of a policeman with whom I had served at Strensford some years earlier. She waved at me from the window and I acknowledged her as Claude checked the tickets. When everyone was seated, he prepared to set off and so I wandered across for a friendly chat.

"Now, Claude," I peered into the loaded coach. "Where are you off to?"

"It's a mystery tour, Mr Rhea, I can't reveal trade secrets."

"The other mystery tour operators allus told us where we were going!" shouted an old lady from inside. "I don't like not knowing where I'm off to."

"Aye, well, this is a proper mystery tour," retorted Claude. "Nobody knows where we're going, that way we can't get lost, eh? But I'll tell you what, you're going somewhere to see somebody that'll give you summat to talk about for years."

I could see from the mutterings in the body of the coach that the passengers weren't over thrilled with this unhelpful information from a driver they'd never experienced until now, but they sat tight as Claude started the engine, closed the door and drove away. For most of them, anything was better than sitting at home alone, even a mystery tour with Claude Jeremiah Greengrass in charge. Mrs Brown waved farewell to me as I watched the departure with interest, knowing from Arnold about Claude's plans.

When Claude returned to Ashfordly, I was still on duty and found myself sorting out a major problem with his busload of passengers.

But to put the story in its sequence and before I was presented with Claude's dilemma, I will recount the story as revealed by Mrs Brown; it was she who later told me what had gone wrong at Scarborough. A day or two after the memorable event, she spotted me patrolling in Ashfordly and came across for a chat, still chuckling about that day out. In her opinion, the day had gone really well; she had thoroughly enjoyed herself. Everything had been fine during the earlier part of the tour; the fish-and-chip lunch in Strensford had been good, but then Claude had driven to the Futurist Theatre on the seafront at Scarborough, arriving about 2.15 p.m. The road outside the theatre was packed with people, all sightseers who were hoping for a glimpse of the arriving stars and the police were having a struggle to control the exuberant crowd.

Claude had parked outside to disgorge his passengers, calling to them as they left the bus, "Mind you wait outside the stage door to see who you should be seeing . . . half an hour you've got, then it's back on board. I'll be here, waiting . . ."

"What are we going to look at?" one old gentleman had asked.

"It says on that notice board the Beatles are here." One lady had pointed to the huge posters outside the theatre.

"What do I want to come and look at beetles for?" grunted one old fellow as he had struggled down the steps of the coach. "I've a garden full of the damned things and them pellets won't shift 'em."

"My daughter says they all want haircuts," another had said.

"Hairy beetles? I've never seen a hairy beetle."

It was evident that few had realised the historic importance of what they were about to witness, but as the last person left the bus, a policeman had arrived.

"You can't park here, sir," he had said to Claude. "No parking here today, there's a coach-park further along, in Valley Road," and he had pointed in the intended direction.

"But I've a load of pensioners out there!" Claude had insisted. "I've got to pick 'em up when they've seen the Beatles."

"And so have lots of other coaches, sir." The policeman had been firm. "Several coachloads of people have arrived to see the Beatles come to their rehearsal, you're not the only one. Now, if you park where I suggest and come back in half an hour, you'll enable other coaches to drop their passengers and we won't finish up with a traffic jam."

And so Claude had obeyed, shouting to his departing load, "I'll be back in half an hour . . ."

Half an hour later, Claude had joined the queue of buses awaiting their passengers and eventually, his party had returned. Chattering noisily about their experience, and the lack of toilets or somewhere for a cup of tea, the excited passengers had eventually settled down as Claude had motored away. I was in Ashfordly marketplace, about to end my period of patrol duty there, when I noticed the return of Claude's bus. He eased to a smooth halt and opened the door; I stood by, eager to know if everyone had enjoyed their mystery tour. As the first lady came to the steps, she turned to Claude and said, "Where are we now, driver?"

"Home," Claude replied. "We're back home now."

"But this isn't Driffield?" she retorted.

"Driffield? Who said we were going to Driffield? This is Ashfordly."

"But I don't live in Ashfordly, I live in Driffield. We all live in Driffield. Is this part of the tour, then? A visit to Ashfordly Castle?"

"No, it's not part of the tour," Claude snapped. "The tour's over. The mystery has been solved, the answer was the Beatles. You went to see the Beatles. We're back home now."

"You might be back home, but we're not," shouted a man from inside the coach. "Besides, you're not our driver! I can see that now you're facing us . . . he wasn't a bit like you from the front. Mind, he needed a haircut an' all."

Claude noticed my presence just outside the bus and, blinking with some embarrassment, asked, "Can you sort this lot out, Mr Rhea? I'm not in Driffield, am I? Can you explain that to 'em?"

"No, Claude, this is Ashfordly. You've got that bit right." I climbed into the bus to address the passengers. "So," I asked them, "where are you all from?"

"Driffield," responded several. "We're on a mystery tour; we've been to Scarborough to see the Beatles. See 'em, not listen to 'em, that is."

"Then you've got on to the wrong bus at Scarborough," I said. Turning to Claude, I repeated that statement. "Claude, you've brought the wrong busload home."

"But I am in the right bus!" he snapped. This is Arnold's bus, isn't it?"

Then I realised what had gone wrong.

"It is Arnold's bus," I agreed. "His new bus! But it's still in the blue colours of the chap he bought it from; Arnold hasn't had time to change the livery," I said, walking to the rear. "It wouldn't surprise me if it still has the previous owner's name on the back!"

And it had. The legend on the back of the bus said "Brougham's Char-a-banc Company" with a Driffield address. I returned to the door of the bus and asked the lady who stood on the top of the steps.

"Was your bus trip arranged with Brougham's?"

"Aye," she said. "It allus is. We allus uses Ted Brougham's buses; he fixed this mystery tour."

"Well, the mystery tour's not over I said," and explained what had happened. "Claude, keep them here for a few minutes, get them to go into the café for a cup of tea and a bit of cake or something. I'll ring Brougham's from the police station and explain what's happened. I reckon you're in for a nice trip to Driffield."

"Driffield? But that'll take all my profit from this trip? And who's paying for those cups of tea?" he asked, as the pensioners made for the café in the marketplace.

"I'm sure you can sort something out, Claude," I grinned. "And make sure they all go to the toilet before they set off, otherwise you'll be stopping behind every convenient hedge between here and the Yorkshire Wolds."

Ted Brougham was very relieved to hear from me. His driver had delivered to Driffield a busload of passengers who said they'd come from Ashfordly and they were now in a café having a cup of tea and a cake. He had no idea where his own passengers had gone, although, from enquiries he'd since made, he guessed they had been delivered to Ashfordly. But he had no point of contact there. We agreed that each coach should set off for the exchange journey in half-an-hours' time along a predetermined route. This meant they would meet halfway between Driffield and Ashfordly and swap passengers. Malton was almost exactly halfway and so it was decided that the exchange would occur in the marketplace at Malton.

"Be careful, Claude, make sure your lot get back on the right bus, we don't want the Driffield folks coming back here again!"

"This is going to cost me a fortune in extra fuel, Mr Rhea, Arnold won't be at all pleased . . ."

But the respective busloads were delighted. When they arrived at Malton, there was an old-time tea-dance in the Milton Rooms and so they all disappeared inside for a waltz or two, with more cups of tea and cakes, before finally returning home. As Mrs Brown said to me afterwards, "By, that was a real good mystery tour, Mr Rhea, like a party it was. We went to places I never knew existed. I mean, I've never been to Driffield in my life and I did enjoy that tea-dance at Malton. I danced with some lovely chaps from Driffield, but I waltzed my heart out with Mr Penniston. He's a real good dancer, you know, and he wants to take me to the next dance, but I've no idea why we went to that theatre at Scarborough. That was a real waste of time, we didn't do anything, we only saw a crowd of people making a lot of noise, shouting and screaming and blocking the road. I never saw any of the Beatles. Unless it was so we would all be made to get on the wrong bus as a surprise, eh? That's the way to run mystery tours, Mr Rhea. Make folks think they've got on the wrong buses!"

"I'll have a word with Arnold Merryweather about it," I assured her.

* * *

In the early 1960s, the roads of England underwent a massive change which included the introduction of motorways. Modelled on the Italian autostrada and the German autobahn, construction of our motorways was authorised by section 11 of the Highways Act of 1959, which called them "special roads". In 1959, 80 miles of motorway were constructed and the Motorways Traffic Regulations of that year laid down the rules for driving on motorways.

One item of interest is that there was no general speed limit on motorways in their early days, although vehicles drawing some types of trailer were restricted to 40 mph. In 1960, a further 45.5 miles of motorway were built with 22 miles in 1961, 52.5 in 1962, 93.5 in 1963, a mere 15.5 miles in 1964 followed by a steady increase in the number of completed motorway miles for the remainder of the 1960s. In spite of protests that they would harm the environment, more motorway miles were completed in the 1970s — and the work continues.

This and other dramatic changes to our system of roads scarcely affected the people of the North York Moors where roundabouts, traffic lights, filter systems and advisory road markings were almost unknown. Even now, as I write these notes in 1995, I am many miles from a set of traffic lights. Way back in the genial 1960s, however, the people of the moors pottered along their lovely lanes blissfully unaware of the dramatic changes being wrought upon the highways in other parts of England. One example of this occurred when a farmer, driving a tractor along the road near Aidensfield, suddenly turned right without any form of signal and entered a farmyard. This caused a motorist behind him to brake suddenly and swerve into a ditch, whereupon the motorist bounded out of his car to vent his feelings upon the tractor driver. The farmer said, in all honesty, "But I always turn in here, I live here." Clearly, that was something the visiting driver should have known!

As our road system began to change, roundabouts were constructed on some main roads which bordered the moors, the roads were subjected to new designs and markings, traffic lights began to appear at crossroads, junctions and upon pedestrian crossings in towns and complicated new requirements for driving emerged.

Nonetheless, very little changed at Aidensfield, other than the occasional repair to a pothole or the clearing of a blocked drain. As a consequence, when the drivers of Aidensfield ventured beyond their normal limits, they found a driver's life fraught with some difficulty. Double roundabouts, filter traffic lights, multi-lane approaches to towns, overhead signals, lane discipline and traffic signs with pictures on them instead of words were all very baffling. Equally baffling were the road signs which appeared when work was being undertaken on the major roads — diversions, contraflow systems, tiers of traffic lights, white lines, yellow lines and yellow crisscross stripes in the middle of the road. Everything seemed designed to cause confusion.

In the early days of Claude Jeremiah Greengrass's work in Arnold Merryweather's bus, there was a lot of change to the major roads which were not far beyond the boundaries of the moors. Road-widening schemes were added with dual carriageways being commonplace; some market towns were bypassed, roundabouts and filter roads were added where crossroads had previously existed; roads were straightened out and corners removed while hills and hollows were levelled, all in the name of greater road safety. But the older people, and those with limited driving experience found such conditions very harrowing and the police were constantly having to rescue motorists who found themselves driving in the wrong direction on dual carriageways or abruptly terminating their journey in the middle of a roundabout which had suddenly appeared where crossroads used to be. Some found themselves in places they never intended and one old gentleman even drove to Edinburgh having intended to reach London. He had entered the wrong carriageway on the A1.

It was in the midst of all this modernisation that an enterprising tycoon decided to open a vast indoor shopping complex at Middlesbrough. It was known as the Ironmasters' and General Shopping Centre because it was built near the railway station on the site of the former Ironmasters' and General Exchange, the latter demolished after construction almost a century earlier in 1868. Inevitably, the name of the old centre was abbreviated to IGC, and so the new shopping complex became widely known as the IGSC — the Ironmasters' and General Shopping Centre. It comprised a huge range of shops under one roof, along with a community centre, restaurants, a library and other services. In many ways, it was ahead of its time.

The opening ceremony was a splendid affair with a prize draw allowing members of the public to attend as guests. Organisations within a forty-mile radius were invited to submit their names for the draw some time ahead of the grand opening, each being allowed to bring up to fifty guests if they won.

The names would be entered in the draw and the ten winning organisations would be announced before the event. They, along with their guests, would be given VIP treatment; they would be invited to the opening ceremony at noon and given mementos of the day; lunch with wine would be provided free at 1 p.m., and, most important, they would be allowed the whole afternoon to shop until 5.30 p.m. at half price at any of the stores within the new centre. The centre's beautiful new shops were closed to the general public that afternoon.

And among the names of the ten winning organisations was Aidensfield Women's Institute. This prompted massive excitement in the village, some of the ladies never having visited such a vast shopping complex and certainly not as a VIP. The secretary had no trouble recruiting fifty ladies for the outing. She had a word with Arnold Merryweather who said he would provide his newest coach for the day. It was now tastefully decorated in his own tan livery but, as one of Arnold's standby drivers was on holiday, he would have to recruit another. He asked Claude Jeremiah Greengrass to drive the ladies to Middlesbrough and he readily agreed — for a price.

At ten o'clock on the morning of the grand opening ceremony, I was patrolling Aidensfield and noticed the bus parked outside the post office. Although it was in August, it was a cold, miserable day with drizzle and low clouds, but the conditions had not deterred lots of extremely smart ladies with big hats. Equipped with umbrellas and suitably large handbags bulging with plenty of cash, they were climbing on board as Claude fussed over them like a broody hen worrying about its chickens.

"Where to today, Claude?" I asked out of interest, the event having slipped my mind.

"That new shopping centre at Middlesbrough, the IGSC," he beamed. "Our WI's won VIP seats. Even bus drivers get looked after — free lunch and cut-price shopping. That's me. I'm enjoying these driving jobs, Constable, believe me."

"It'll be smashing, shopping indoors on a mucky day like this!" quipped one lady as she climbed aboard.

"Well, have a great day," I wished them well and resumed my patrol. At quarter past ten, the coach chugged past me *en route* to the main road from where it would cruise steadily towards its destination. It was in good time for a noon arrival.

I could not identify any of the ladies on board because all the windows had steamed up due to the drizzle-laden atmosphere outside. Indeed, the drizzle had dampened their overcoats and umbrellas and so the interior of the bus was like a sauna, with steam rising from the wet clothing to coat the interior of the windows. One or two had wiped their windows but visibility from the coach was sadly impaired. For some, this would have been a rare trip across the moors with wonderful views and an opportunity to see places they rarely visited, but the rain had frustrated a lot of hopes. In spite of that, I felt sure the happiness and excitement of the occasion at IGSC — plus the opportunity for cut-price shopping — would more than compensate. Having watched the bus depart, I went home for my morning coffee.

The remainder of that morning was very quiet with little to occupy me, and when lunchtime came, it was something of a relief from the monotony. It was 12.30 and I was just finishing my meal, having chatted with Mary and the children, when the telephone rang. It was the secretary of the proprietor of IGSC at Middlesbrough.

"PC Rhea, Aidensfield Police," I announced myself.

"Oh, good afternoon, Constable. I'm sorry to bother you over this — it might be nothing, but I felt I should check and didn't know who to contact." She was very apologetic. "But Mr Vaughan, that's my boss, thinks I should make a few calls."

"Well, tell me what the problem is, and I'll see what I can do," I offered.

She explained about the opening ceremony at Middlesbrough and how various organisations had been drawn as guests, including Aidensfield WI.

"The snag is, Constable, the Aidensfield ladies haven't arrived. We are all waiting to start, you see, expecting them, but don't like to begin without them. I don't know the name of the WI secretary, or the coach proprietor, and so I rang you."

"Well," I said, "the WI secretary's on the bus, I saw her get on, so you can't contact her. However, I can definitely say they set off this morning. I saw them. A busload of ladies with full purses and big hats. They left here about quarter past ten and should have been at your centre by now. They should have got to Middlesbrough by eleven-thirty or so; certainly they've had enough time to park and reach you."

"Yes, that's what Mr Vaughan thought. He wondered if something has gone wrong. I mean, should we start without them? We are delayed now, actually, we should have begun at twelve but felt we could hang on a while, just in case."

I groaned. With Claude Jeremiah Greengrass at the wheel, anything could have happened. I knew that if the coach had been involved in an accident, I should have known — buses which were full of passengers and involved in accidents were always headline news, but I said I would check with Arnold Merryweather, with my divisional headquarters, with my own Force control room and those of Middlesbrough Borough Police and County Durham, and with local hospitals, the AA and the RAC, just to be sure.

I asked her to wait just a little longer, and I would get back to her. I spent the next half-hour on the telephone, ringing all the likely places, but no one had come across Arnold Merryweather's bus or its passengers. Arnold had not had word from Claude to say there was a problem, and the bus did not seem to have been involved in a traffic accident. No one from it had been taken into any of the hospitals for treatment, and none of the emergency services had any information about a broken-down bus full of WI members. I decided to ring IGSC and suggest they begin their celebrations without the Aidensfield contingent.

While I was on the phone, Arnold came around to my house looking very flustered and worried. I completed my call to IGSC, assuring the secretary that we had heard nothing to suggest the bus or any of its passengers had been involved in an accident, and we could only guess it had suffered a breakdown.

"I suggest you start without them," I told her. "They could still arrive in time for lunch, and certainly there's time to get a bus repaired before the shopping finishes. If I do hear anything, I'll get in touch with you."

"Thank you, Mr Rhea, but what a disappointment for them."

"It might not be as bad as we think," I tried to reassure her.

She thanked me and I rang off as Arnold grew more and more agitated with the delay.

"What can have happened, Nick? If they'd broken down, Claude would have rung by now, surely?" He was normally a calm individual, a bespectacled man in his early sixties with a mop of dark, well-groomed hair and dark, warm eyes. Now he was very worried. Arnold was always well dressed, even when driving one of his buses, and for a bachelor, took great care over his appearance.

"A puncture?" I suggested. "Claude's maybe got a local garage to fix it. It all takes time."

"Aye, things can take a long time to get sorted out, but this is most unusual. I mean, a bus can't disappear from the face of the earth, can it? Not with a load of women going shopping!"

I felt like saying it could vanish if Claude was driving, but resisted adding to Arnold's worries by explaining the checks I had made. I assured him that if any of the organisations I had spoken to received further information, they would contact me. I'd be the first to know if there had been a calamity of any kind. Arnold thought he should contact the families of the missing women, but I resisted that.

"No, that would spread undue alarm," I said. "There's no real concern yet; we know there's not been an accident and that no one is hurt, so don't get the families involved, Arnold. We don't want to start a panic. Besides, if they were due to go shopping until half past five, you can reckon six o'clock before they get back on the bus, then an hour and a half to get back here, plus a stop of three quarters of an hour for a drink . . . you'd not expect them back in Aidensfield before quarter past eight. There's loads of time for things to get sorted out and for us to be told of any problem, if indeed there is one."

I suggested that Arnold return to his office to take any incoming phone calls — after all, if there was a problem, Claude would surely ring Arnold, so it was important that he was available to answer his telephone. He did as I suggested, and I then resumed my patrol after acquainting Mary with the details; if anyone called my office in my absence, she would contact me via my radio.

During the afternoon, I popped into Arnold's office to see if he had received any further news, and he shook his head. He looked grey with worry and was clearly very concerned. "I've been on to all sorts of folks I know in my line of business between here and Middlesbrough — garages, bus depots, breakdown recoveries — they've heard nowt, Mr Rhea. I rang that shopping centre an' all, and Claude's not turned up yet. His passengers have missed the opening and the lunch, and all the other guests are in the shops now, spending up to their eyeballs — all except my busload. Where the hell can he have got to?"

I looked at my watch. It was four o'clock and the weather was still extremely dull. The drizzle had not let up during the day and the overall gloominess had persisted with the threat of fog now being forecast. It was more like a day in February than a day in summer.

"It is possible they have arrived and not been noticed," I said. "I mean, Arnold, there's five hundred women there at least — if Claude has bypassed the booking-in system, they might be there now, unnoticed among all the others and having a whale of a time."

"And if they're not? Then what?"

"I might have to arrange a search party," I heard myself saying. "But a busload of people isn't like a child getting lost or somebody stealing a car." Then I had a thought. "Did Claude take a map?" I asked Arnold.

"No, he said he knew his way to Middlesbrough, and the new centre is well signed once he gets there. I said he could take one of my road atlases, but he said he didn't need it. Besides, IGSC has erected signs on all the approach roads, for the buses they were expecting from all over the north-east."

"If I am to arrange a search," I said, "we'd need something more important than a busload of women going shopping and who've simply failed to turn up. You know as well as me that when some women get into the shops, they lose all sense of time. They could have decided to go somewhere else. The lack of news about them convinces me they're safe, Arnold, so there's very little reason to get other police involved. If your bus has crashed or if someone is hurt or has had to be rushed into hospital, we should have known by now."

"Old Miss Talbot needs regular attention, something to do with her waterworks," smiled Arnold. "We could say she needs medical attention and we're getting worried."

"Right," I decided against my better judgement. "I'll see about putting an 'All Stations' out for the bus."

An "All Stations" message was one which was circulated by radio to every police station in England and Wales. There were varying grades of message, the most important being an Express Message; this was issued when a murder or other serious crime had been committed, for example. All Ports Warnings were issued for escaped prisoners or criminals thought to be attempting a flight overseas, but a busload of potential shoppers who had not gone shopping was hardly the material for such an alert. Nonetheless, I rang Sergeant Blaketon to put forward my proposal. As expected, he resisted.

"Rhea," he snapped, "you cannot waste police time and resources searching for a busload of women shoppers who are in the supposed care of Greengrass. There are no reports of accidents and injuries and no search requests from worried relatives. I can't imagine that they have been kidnapped or spirited off to Mars. You know what women are, Rhea: they'll be shopping; they'll be having a knees-up somewhere."

I played my trump card. I mentioned Mrs Talbot's waterworks.

"All right," Blaketon capitulated after I had elaborated upon her supposed embarrassing condition. "Arrange an 'All Stations' asking routine patrols to look out for the bus and, if seen, to provide you with its location and condition. A non-urgent enquiry, I suggest, Rhea, no criminal offences suspected. Stress that we have no reason to believe that the Greengrass Express and all those aboard have been kidnapped or that they have become victims of a highway robbery. This is a humanitarian gesture, aid to a damsel in distress."

"Very good, Sergeant." And so I provided details of Arnold's bus, with the all-important registration number. Sergeant Blaketon would initiate the "All Stations" message with my name and telephone number as the contact. With a spot of luck and some good police observation, we might find now Arnold's bus and its passengers.

Before releasing the message, I made a final check with IGSC in Middlesbrough, but the Aidensfield ladies had not arrived, nor had the centre received any messages from Claude. The secretary was sure of that because all the seats had been reserved with the name of the group concerned, and tickets were issued to each guest to allow them the discounted shopping. In Aidensfield's case, none had been taken. I told Blaketon that none of the families had been alerted to the absence of their shopping ladies, and he thought that wise; after all, no one wanted an unnecessary panic with the inevitable publicity and there was plenty of time for the missing people to turn up safe and sound. And we did know — or at least we were fairly certain — there had been no reported accident to the bus or injuries to its passengers.

"I don't suppose the bus could have rolled down an embankment into a gulley or gone off the road into a river or driven off a bridge into the Tees without anyone noticing?" was Blaketon's later reaction.

"It's hardly likely," I responded, knowing that such things could indeed happen. I knew that a coach might run off one of our moorland roads and roll down a steep slope, probably to remain in a remote gulley for some time before discovery, but it was most unlikely. I put my trust in Greengrass — that trust was not so much a belief in his integrity, but a knowledge that he was likely, even in these circumstances, to do something stupid. If he had, his lapse would be discovered. I hoped our "All Stations" would soon provide the answer which in fact it did.

An August meeting was underway at Redcar Races and, like all racecourses, it was equipped with a small temporary police station. A contingent of officers was on duty at the races, consequently the office was staffed for the duration of the meeting.

When the "All Stations" was circulated, it included that temporary police office and details of the missing bus were distributed to all police officers on duty at the racecourse. Six of them had the task of patrolling the coach-parks, and so details of Arnold's bus were given to those men. And they found the bus. It was parked among hundreds of other coaches and was quite empty.

My telephone rang shortly after 5 p.m.

"It's Chalky White speaking from Redcar Races," said the voice. "I've found your missing bus — it's here, on the racecourse, empty."

"Empty? Is the driver with it?" I asked. I'd known PC White for years.

"No, nobody," he said. "So, what now, Nick? The bus is safe."

"It's the passengers I'm worried about," and I explained what had happened. Chalky wondered if the driver had dropped his passengers off near the new IGSC complex before bringing his bus here, to give himself a day at the races while the women enjoyed their outing.

"That sounds like the sort of trick Greengrass would play," I agreed, but added, "but the IGSC people say none of the women turned up either."

"They'll be here, Nick, having a whale of a time. I shouldn't worry about it anymore if I were you. We've had no reports of accidents, injuries or sickness, so I reckon you can relax now."

"Do one thing for me, Chalky," I asked, because I wanted to know the full story. "Put a tannoy message out, will you? Ask Mr Greengrass, the driver of Merryweather's Coach, to telephone me at home as soon as possible, certainly before he leaves the course," I said, and provided the number in case Greengrass claimed he couldn't remember it.

"Sure," agreed Chalky White. "The last race is due in five minutes, I'll tannoy your request when the winner has been declared and before the Tote pay-out is announced. That'll be the best time to get people's attention."

I thanked him and then rang Arnold Merryweather with the news.

"Redcar Races?" he exploded. "What the hell's he doing there?"

"I think his passengers are there too," I said. "I'm awaiting a call from Claude."

"It's the last time that idiot drives for me!" snapped Arnold, slamming down the telephone.

I rang Blaketon too, to say that the coach had been located at Redcar with no sign of being involved in an accident.

"Whereabouts at Redcar?" was his obvious question.

"The races," I said.

"I might have known!" he shouted down the handset. "Put that maniac Greengrass in charge of anything and it goes wrong. What in the name of Camarero is he doing at Redcar Races?"

"I don't know. I've left a message for him to call me," was all I could offer by way of explanation and after listening to Sergeant Blaketon's language of anger and frustration, I replaced the telephone. Next, I rang IGSC to inform Mr Vaughan that the coach had been traced to Redcar Races, albeit with no explanation yet as to why it had gone to Redcar instead of Middlesbrough.

I did express the view that none of the ladies was injured or harmed in any way and added that Mr Merryweather would surely apologise to Mr Vaughan for the upset he had caused on their important day.

At six o'clock my telephone rang. It was Claude Jeremiah and he sounded as if he had had far too much to drink. I decided to attempt a sobering-up exercise by frightening him and said, "Claude, there's been a nationwide police search for you this afternoon. 'All Stations' messages have been flashing between Aidensfield and New Scotland Yard . . ."

"Search? For me? What have I done now?"

"You kidnapped a busload of passengers," I snapped. "You were supposed to go to Middlesbrough."

He was a little more sober now, and said, "Aye, but we got lost, you see. All them roadworks and traffic signs and lights on the A19 as you approach Middlesbrough, and what with my window being steamed up and no one on board knowing which was the right way, well, I finished up at Redcar."

"You could have still got to Middlesbrough!" I snapped. "Redcar's not far away!"

"Aye, well, it wasn't quite so easy, Mr Rhea, you see. I didn't know we were in Redcar, there was nowt to say we weren't in Middlesbrough, all the streets and roads join up, not like us in the country with miles between villages. Then we got into this long queue of buses and there were signs with GSIC and arrows pointing along the road saying 'GSIC — coach-park'. So, well, I thought I was on the right road and heading for the right place."

"Well, if you'd followed those signs properly you'd have got to the right place!" I cried.

"That's what I thought, Constable," he chuckled now. "But GSIC means General Shires Insurance Company not that funny name for the new shopping complex. That's IGSC, you see, I was following GSIC . . ."

I groaned. This could only happen to Greengrass.

"Anyroad," he said, "this chap asked if my bus was full of official guests and I said it was, and so we were all taken into a posh suite at the racecourse, along with lots of other folks in smart suits and posh frocks. There was champagne and wine and drinks and food and more drinks and more champagne and more food and then it was time for the races and so we all had a bet or two . . . well, Constable, I can tell you that my ladies didn't want to go shopping, not after all that. Most had never been racing before, some of 'em won a fortune, Mr Rhea, and they've all had a wonderful day out for nowt . . . it's not cost us a penny, except for a bit of betting money."

"You could have told somebody where you were, Claude, IGSC were frantic; they had seats reserved for you and thought there'd been an accident."

"I never thought we'd be missed, Constable, I mean, it was just a big do in a shopping centre for hundreds of women . . . I had no idea anybody would miss us."

I told him about the police search and the worries, and the anguish in poor old Arnold, and then said, "And I'm going to leave your name on our search list for another few hours. That means if any police officer sees that bus on your drive back home, you'll be stopped and quizzed — so you'd better make sure you are sober before you set off, or get Arnold to come for you . . ."

The bus did arrive home at the anticipated time. It was driven by Miss Esme Railton, a former wartime WRAC lorry driver, and so none of the families of the WI ladies were ever alarmed by their absence.

But I think a lot of husbands wondered how on earth their wives could visit a brand-new shopping centre to be given half-price discount, and yet return home with more money than they had set off with.

Claude was not asked to drive any more buses for Arnold Merryweather, but Esme Railton, a lady who had once courted Arnold in his younger days, did find herself with a new part-time job. She became Arnold's new driver and I understand Hannah was not very pleased about that!

7. GREENGRASS INTOXICATED

Man, being reasonable, must get drunk.
LORD BYRON, 1788–1824

The history and purpose of the nation's liquor-licensing laws makes interesting reading but we can believe erroneously that existing restrictions have always been in force. In fact, they haven't. The laws governing the *sale* of intoxicating liquor are comparatively modern, although some early attempts were made to govern excess consumption and drunkenness. For many generations, drunkenness was regarded as the sin of gluttony and to teach their children about its evils, the ancient Lacedaemonians used to get their slaves drunk and show the results to their children "to give them an aversion and a horror of the vice". The legacy of the sinfulness of being drunk meant that in England drunkenness was punishable by the ecclesiastical courts but by 4 Jac.1 c.5 and 21 Jac.1 c.7 the justices could impose a penalty for anyone found drunk — they were fined five shillings for their first offence. Failure to pay the fine led to six hours in the stocks. A second offence meant a fine of £10 — a huge sum at that time, certainly much more than a year's wages for a labourer.

Today, drunkenness, in itself, is not an offence against criminal law although one old statute of James I referred to the "odious crime of drunkenness". In Britain, anyone can become drunk at home without breaking the criminal law; indeed, there are no age restrictions on children drinking at home (the under-18 rule refers to the bars of licensed premises) but drunkenness becomes an offence when certain other factors are involved. These include being in charge of something like a bull, a loaded firearm, a child under seven years of age or a motor vehicle, or being drunk in places like cafés, inns, billiard halls or on-board passenger steamers.

Ale has long been sold and consumed in this country as part of our diet, this drink for centuries being safer than a polluted water supply and, in times past, our common law imposed no restrictions on the selling of intoxicants. It was The Alehouse Act of 1828 which formed the basis of the modern rules which govern the sale and supply of intoxicants through a system of licenses for inns, alehouses and victualling houses; successive legislation has perpetuated the system, albeit with changes. One important piece of legislation was the Licensing Act of 1872, parts of which were still in force when I joined the police. Sections of it had then been superseded by many other statutes even though some portions remained effective.

In its original form, this old Act imposed restrictions on the hours of opening of licensed premises and restricted the times of the sale of intoxicants but it also created a range of offences involving drunkenness. Drunk in charge of a carriage on the highway or in any public place was one example, as was being drunk in charge of horses, cattle, pigs, sheep and steam engines. The offences of being drunk and incapable, or drunk and disorderly in a public place were also incorporated within that Act. Other offences in the 1902 Licensing Act included prohibiting the sale of intoxicants to habitual drunkards, and this Act also provided various powers of arrest to police officers.

Although the 1990s have seen a relaxation of the rules governing the sale and consumption of intoxicants, the sale of alcoholic drinks in Britain continues to be rigorously controlled, both by excise licenses and justices' licenses. These restrictions arose during the last century because children, some as young as two years of age, were dying of illnesses associated with the consumption of intoxicants, particularly spirits such as gin. In 1908, a two-year-old died of cirrhosis of the liver and there was a popular notice in inns which said, *Drunk for a penny, dead drunk for two pence. Straw free.* Drinking and prostitution were rife among ten- and twelve-year-old girls early last century but it wasn't until 1901 that the law forbade the sale of intoxicating liquor to children under fourteen. Even so, children below that age could buy amounts of one pint or less if it was in a sealed and corked container, the theory being they would take it home to mum or dad with the seal unbroken.

Any police officer can tell wonderful stories of dealing with happy drunks, but troublesome drunks or violent drunks do not provide such interesting or memorable work. Sadly, over-indulgence in intoxicants sometimes turns normal, pleasant young men into raving lunatics who want to fight everyone and who often end their binge in the cold, dark and highly sobering influence of a police cell, or sometimes in a hospital. Others perform stupid acts while under the influence of beer or spirits such as climbing church steeples, stealing flags from town halls, balancing along the parapets of bridges at dangerous heights, driving railway engines without authority, invading hotels and hospitals for a bit of "fun" to cheer up the residents or patients, or attempting to change the decor of a town centre by removing flowers from municipal gardens and replanting them in obscure places like factory gates or waste metal dumps. The ingenuity of some drunks is quite remarkable. Some display more inventiveness when drunk than they do when sober. Maybe alcohol improves or stimulates parts of the brain?

Years ago, there was a charming old drunk in York. He was utterly harmless and always cheerful, yet on frequent occasions he could be found littering the city centre after serious drinking sessions in his favourite pub. He would find himself arrested for being drunk and incapable in a street or public place, hauled before the magistrates and fined something like ten shillings (50p). He had more than 400 such arrests to his credit as a consequence of which he became such an expert in the arrest procedure at a police station, that all the newly appointed constables would practise on him. Whenever he was discovered in his oft-inebriated state, any newly appointed constable, still wet behind the ears and in need of practical experience, would be sent to arrest him. After being placed in the cells to sober up, our helpful drunkard would then guide the constable through the complexities of the arrest procedure — and a very good tutor he was too. He took each nervous constable through the steps one by one until the task was satisfactorily concluded. Sometimes I wish he could have been rewarded for his tutorship of young constables. Maybe they could have bought him a drink?

Claude Jeremiah Greengrass was not so helpful. Claude was not a habitual drunkard however, nor did he become violent or abusive after a session in the pub. If he had had far too much to drink, he would simply go to sleep — this could happen anywhere. On various occasions, he was found snoozing in the gents' toilets, snoring in a corner of the bar, slumbering in a pigsty, napping among George's new tulips and reposing beside a milk stool in the byre of a nearby farm. A surfeit of alcohol invariably knocked him out — a most satisfactory outcome since instead of becoming belligerent, he would lapse into a deep sleep.

However, if he had had just a little too much to drink, he was liable to remain awake and do silly things — one New Year's Eve he decided to play the bagpipes in the main street of Aidensfield at 2 a.m., which did not endear him to the local population, and on another he decided to hoist a flag on top of the village hall at 3 a.m. but fell off the ladder he had borrowed from a builder's yard. He landed head first in the village horse trough whereupon he sobered up fairly quickly, particularly as Sergeant Blaketon, on a night patrol, happened to arrive as he was extracting himself from the trough.

He was almost charged with stealing the ladder but managed to persuade Blaketon that he had borrowed it to look for a leak in the roof. Not really believing Claude's excuse, Sergeant Blaketon had enjoyed the sight of Claude's indignity in the trough and, later, the owner of the ladder said he would have given Claude permission to use it had he asked, although such permission might not have been readily given at three o'clock in the morning.

It was this propensity for silly alcohol-induced behaviour that resulted in Claude's appearance at Ashfordly Magistrates Court on several occasions. Invariably, he could not be charged with being drunk and disorderly because that implied some kind of ruffian behaviour such as fighting or causing damage, nor could we consider a charge of being drunk and incapable because he was capable of doing things, even if they were extremely stupid.

One example concerned an adventure with a pogo stick. During his multifarious dealings in junk, Claude had acquired a second-hand pogo stick from a retired circus performer. He had been told that the pogo stick had once been owned by the world-famous clown, The Great Garibaldi, and that he had broken the world record on that very instrument in 1938, amassing a total of 101,101 jumps without placing a foot on the ground. Claude had believed the story, and went around telling everyone that The Great Garibaldi had actually owned this very stick, long before these sticks became so popular in the 1970s.

Having bought the pogo stick, Claude thought it would be rather useful. Although pogo sticks are known to have existed as early as 1921, they reached their peak of popularity in Britain in the craze of the early 1970s when everyone seemed to be jumping on them and using them as means of transport. A pogo stick comprises a single metal shaft with footrests some six inches off the ground at either side; a powerful spring is concealed within the hollow shaft near the base and to the bottom of the spring is attached a strong rubber ferrule. In its relaxed mode, the spring protrudes and is compressed into the shaft when anyone climbs aboard. Users leap on to the footrests and, through skill in keeping their balance, can proceed in large, spring-assisted kangaroo-type hops on this one-legged stilt. A competent pogo-stick jumper can cover a large distance in a short time, or can remain in the same place while jumping up and down — a very useful activity. Indeed, in 1985, the record for pogo-stick jumping was established in America. A man managed 130,077 jumps in March of that year, but he probably performed all these in one place.

All this happened some years after Claude's acquisition. Having purchased this interesting object, Claude found he could not sell it — among the people of Aidensfield, there was little demand for pogo sticks, even those with long and famous histories. If he was to sell it, he decided that he must be capable of demonstrating its facilities and so, for a while, he practised in what he hoped was the seclusion of his ranch. People did see him in action, however, and according to some eye-witnesses, he soon became very proficient on his one-legged stilt. He used it to trek across the moors, to visit his hen run and to shepherd his flock of sheep. Then, in a fit of bravado having achieved some success on board his pogo stick, he decided to ride it to the pub. Upon arrival, he parked it in the umbrella stand.

Having enjoyed a drink or two, and faced with the trip home in the dark, Claude wondered whether he needed a white light to the front of his stick and a red light to the rear if he was to take it on the public highway. As there was no sign of my presence in the street, the slightly inebriated Claude leapt aboard to execute a short journey of several hops before returning to earth with a bump. He found it difficult to control the pogo stick when he was full of beer; the stick fell over and, even when it remained upright, it refused to proceed in a straight line.

Clearly, he needed more practice and as he worked on his new hobby, his unique skill became the talking point in the pub. Claude responded with a well-rehearsed history of the stick, stressing that it was world-famous as well as being a record-holder. It wasn't long before someone bet Claude that he could not hop a specified distance along Aidensfield's main street aboard his new toy.

One warm evening in late summer, the regulars in the bar began to ply him with free beer as the challenge grew stronger. By half past nine, the challenge had been accepted by a well-oiled Claude. It was quite simple — on board his rubber-ferruled pogo stick, he had to hop along the street from outside the pub to a point opposite the post office. It wasn't very far — perhaps a hundred yards at the most — but for Claude to win the bet, he had to cover the entire distance without putting either foot on the ground. Having spent hours practising at home, he felt completely confident that he would win the bet — if he did win, £5 would come his way from wagers collected by George Ward, the landlord; if he lost, he had to buy drinks all round.

At the appointed time, the crowd of about two dozen regulars trooped out of the pub and gathered around as Claude had a couple of extra drinks before setting off. The light had almost faded and darkness was beginning to envelope Aidensfield, so the assembly around the pogo stick passed unnoticed by most of the villagers. On the street outside the pub and surrounded by his fans, Claude was in need of great encouragement if he was to attempt this feat; after all, successful completion would be an achievement never before accomplished in the history of the world.

"Ready, Claude?" asked George, when Claude had sunk a third pint of courage to the resounding cheers of the assembled witnesses.

"As ready as I ever shall be," muttered Claude, his words slightly slurred by this stage.

"Right, when I shout 'go', get aboard that stick of yours and set off. You've got to reach the post office without putting a foot down. God knows how you're going to steer that thing so watch out for cars and buses; remember you haven't any lights and it hasn't any brakes either, but I suppose you know how to control it."

"There's only me knows how to control it, I'm the expert and I don't need a steering wheel," muttered Claude. "Have you got that five quid set aside for me?"

"I have, so your money's guaranteed. All you have to do is get to the post office without stopping and without putting a foot down. Ready?"

"Aye," murmured Claude, without much enthusiasm.

It was about this time that Sergeant Blaketon entered the village in his official police motor car with me in the passenger seat. We were executing an evening tour of all the licensed premises on my beat, a chore that Sergeant Blaketon liked to perform with me about twice a year. This was our final call. We had our sidelights burning as we cruised slowly along the street, Blaketon alert as always for bikes and cars travelling without their obligatory lights.

"It's been a very quiet evening, Rhea," he said with some pride. "I must say that your motorists all obey the lighting regulations and you keep all your licensed premises in good order. All very well conducted, if I may say so."

I was tempted to remind him that they were not "my" motorists nor "my" licensed premises, but my words would have made little or no impact because he held me responsible for whatever happened on Aidensfield beat. I told him that I rarely had problems with the local motorists and that I was fortunate in the landlords who ran the pubs — they all kept good houses. As we drove through Aidensfield, I became aware of a crowd outside the pub. Men were milling around the doorway and, bathed as they were in the light from the interior, it was difficult to see clearly in the exterior darkness but they were loudly cheering something or someone in their midst. They were making quite a lot of noise, but I had no idea what was happening. Blaketon noticed them too.

"What's going on outside the pub, Rhea?" he asked. "Sounds a bit like a riot to me."

"Mebbe they're betting on snails racing across the road," I suggested.

"Betting is not allowed on licensed premises, Rhea, so I think we should investigate," was his reaction to my attempted joke and then the familiar features of Claude Jeremiah Greengrass appeared above the heads of the others, his crown of thin white hair highlighted in the glow from the premises. I groaned inwardly. What in the name of Beelzebub was Claude doing now?

"Is that Greengrass on a soap box, Rhea?" Blaketon asked as the car drew closer. "Is he about to make a speech? This I must hear!"

And as we drove nearer, it was eminently clear that the cheering crowd was oblivious to our presence.

Then, as we were preparing to find a parking place in front of the pub, a manoeuvre which meant crossing to the other side of the road, the circle of men suddenly broke ranks and some of them stepped aside as Claude Jeremiah Greengrass burst out of their midst on board his pogo stick. He was concentrating so hard upon the task which faced him, with his eyes looking down at his feet, that he did not see our car as we were in the tricky process of turning across the road. He had no idea that we were moving towards him. With three huge spring-loaded bounds in the space of a split second, he was directly in front of the police car and Sergeant Blaketon did his best to brake, but a collision was inevitable. With a sickening thud, we collided with Claude's stick as he flew forwards and landed on the bonnet with his face pressed against the windscreen. He found himself gazing directly into Sergeant Blaketon's angry glare. We stopped with a squeal of brakes.

"Greengrass, get your filthy self off my bonnet!" shouted the sergeant, bringing the car to a halt and climbing out. "I have just polished that bodywork!"

"Are you hurt, Claude?" I asked with some concern as I hurried to his aid. He slid to the ground and managed to find his feet, then blinked at me and Blaketon; he was swaying slightly, but was not injured in any way.

"That's dangerous driving, that is," he slurred his words. "I'll have you for this, Blaketon, trying to run me down."

"You're drunk!" snapped Blaketon.

"And you're ugly, but I'll be sober in the morning!" snapped Claude. "Now, if you've damaged my pogo stick, the Force will have to pay for its repair. I'll have you know that's a unique instrument, world-famous it is. Renowned in the world of pogo-jumping."

But Sergeant Blaketon was more concerned about damage to the official car. He was closely examining it, knowing that if it had been dented or damaged in any way, he would have to submit a report to headquarters and answer countless questions from his superiors. He knew he would have difficulty in explaining how he came to knock Claude Jeremiah Greengrass off a pogo stick. Fortunately, there was no damage, not even a scratch on the paintwork or a crack in any glass.

"You're very lucky, Greengrass!" he said at length. "This car is not damaged, otherwise I'd have had you . . ."

"Had me? Now hang on, this one's your fault, you ran into me!" Claude was blinking furiously as he struggled to come to terms with the incident. "You knocked me off my stick, and you're on the wrong side of the road an' all . . . that's careless driving, Sergeant Blaketon, and I have half a mind to report you."

"You're drunk, Greengrass!" retorted Blaketon. "You're drunk in charge of that pogo stick!"

"There's no such offence, Sergeant!" grinned Claude. "You can't have me for that!"

"I can. It's a carriage, Greengrass. If a bicycle is a carriage under the Licensing Act of 1872, as determined in Corkery v Carpenter in 1950, then so is your pogo stick. You were on the highway, you were being carried and both feet were off the ground, therefore it is a carriage. And if it is a carriage, it needs lights during the hours of darkness, and brakes . . . I'm reporting you for being drunk in charge of a carriage on the highway. And if you object, I shall have you arrested and taken to Ashfordly Police Station . . ."

I could only stand back in dismay as Sergeant Blaketon read the riot act to the assembled regulars, threatening to summons each of them for aiding and abetting Claude in his foolhardy, illegal act, and criticising George for allowing such conduct on licensed premises, to say nothing of the bets that were being laid.

As the subdued regulars trooped inside, Claude's pogo stick was confiscated.

"Confiscated? You can't confiscate that, it's my property!" Claude shouted.

"It's evidence, Greengrass!" was Blaketon's curt reply. "Evidence for the court."

After experiencing Sergeant Blaketon's wrath, the regulars had all returned to the bar, leaving Claude alone to answer for his behaviour. The unhappy Claude had lost his bet and would now have to buy everyone a drink; George, meanwhile, was beginning to worry about his licence because the conduct of licensed premises was his responsibility. Unruly behaviour, betting on the premises and permitting drunkenness might all put his licence at risk. We drove away without a word.

"Sergeant," I said after a while, "you weren't serious about prosecuting Claude for being drunk in charge of a carriage, were you?"

"That contraption of his is a carriage, Rhea," he retorted. "It is constructed for the carriage of a person and it was upon the highway, therefore it is a carriage. He was in charge of it, and he was drunk. That's all I need — and I have the device in question which can be shown to the court."

But I noticed the gleam in his eye when he dropped me at my police house. He told me to take the pogo stick with me and said, "You keep that thing, Rhea, at least for a few days. I think Claude, George and his pals have suffered enough but keep up the pretence. Let him think I am going to take him to court. Keep him on tenterhooks for a day or two, then give that thing back to him. I don't think he will take it on the highway again, do you?"

"Not without brakes and lights," I answered.

*　*　*

Among the regular haunts of Claude Jeremiah Greengrass were the auction rooms, house and farm sales in and around Aidensfield. He was a familiar figure among the sale-goers because this was his main source of resaleable items. He bought all manner of job lots sometimes stumbling across a valuable object but, more often than not, returning home with a load of old rubbish. Rudolph Burley, the auctioneer, knew Claude very well indeed and if Claude was experiencing a hard time financially, Rudolph would knock down to him a miscellany of lots for a very modest bid or two. It was also a way for Rudolph to get rid of rubbish which no one else would entertain.

It was a brisk March day when all the livestock along with the machinery and equipment, plus the contents of Aud Elijah Barron's farmhouse at Skeugh Heights, Elsinby, were to be sold. Aud Elijah was retiring to a cottage in the village, along with his wife, Annie, and five sheepdogs.

In the North York Moors, the prefix "Aud" is widely used as a term of affection; technically, it means "old", but is seldom used in that context. It is almost a term of endearment and many young men have the prefix "Aud" added to their names. Claude was often known as Aud Claude and I have heard him described at that aud fraud Claude.

When Elijah and Annie's big day arrived, I was on duty at the sale, chiefly to ensure that traffic along the approach roads was not placed at risk from the comings and goings of vehicles when arriving and leaving Skeugh Heights. My presence at the sale was also regarded as useful from the peace-keeping aspect, particularly if any disputes arose. I was well aware of the phrase *caveat emptor* which means "buyer beware". I knew that it was the responsibility of the buyer to inspect the goods before making a bid — for a bid at auction is binding. The full legal maxim is *caveat emptor, qui ignorare non debuit quod ius alienum emit.* Translated, this means: Let a purchaser beware, for he ought not to be ignorant of the nature of the property which he is buying from another party.

Aud Elijah's farm was positioned upon an exposed moorland ridge and access was via a long, winding and ascending track which led from a narrow lane between Elsinby and Ploatby. The livestock sale was in the morning, with viewing at 8 a.m. followed by the sale at 10 a.m.; there was a break from noon until 1.30 p.m., when the machinery and house contents were to be auctioned.

Many local people, including the regular at tenders at such sales, would make a full day of this event, adjourning to the Hopbind Inn for their lunchtime refreshment. The pub was open all afternoon, having been granted an extension of hours by the local magistrates because of the sale. Some people had no intention of purchasing anything — they came for the outing and the distinctive atmosphere of a country sale. Some, of course, came to compare their household rubbish with that on view. But there was not a lot of genuine rubbish at Aud Elijah's; he always bought thoroughly good furniture and equipment and even the animals were of top quality. Well, almost all of them were.

When I was satisfied that most of the incoming vehicles had arrived, I walked up to the farm and through the huge barn where the indoor sale would be conducted. It was about 11.15 and outside at the rear, Rudolph was in full flight, his loud, rapid-fire voice drowning all other sounds as he auctioned a fine herd of dairy Friesians which were in the field behind him. Knowledgeable buyers were there and the herd was a particularly fine one; I saw the animals knocked down at a very fair price to a gentleman farmer from Wensleydale. After a few minutes, I returned through the barn to see if I could find a cup of coffee and *en route* bumped into Claude.

"Now, Claude," I greeted him, "what brings you here?"

"It's nowt to do with the law what I do in my leisure time." He was defensive, as always.

"I was just being polite," I countered, pointing to the furniture which was arrayed about the floor of the barn. "There's some good stuff here, animals and furniture alike. Antiques, very classy ones, if I'm any judge."

"Too posh for me, is the likes of that stuff," he muttered. "I go for the tail-end stuff, Mr Rhea, that way you get bargains. Job lots, boxes of books and crockery, cutlery and glasses . . . and then I sell 'em on."

"Well, I hope you find something useful," I said, leaving him as he wandered into the barn. Behind the barn, Rudolph had now turned to sell the pigs which had been herded into pens; he was selling half a dozen at a time. Some saddlebacks were first to be sold and when all the pigs had gone, it would be the turn of the sheep, black-faced Swaledales, which were also in pens outside. Last on the list of livestock, after the hens, geese and ducks, was Elijah's aud gallower, a Cleveland Bay gelding called Lazarus. He was in the stable, awaiting his destiny. An aud gallower is the local name for a faithful horse; I knew Elijah would be very upset at having to part with his horse, for they had been together for years.

Elijah would ride Lazarus into the village to collect his groceries and his mail and, over the years, the pair had become inseparable. Lazarus was a skinny old animal of indeterminate age; he seemed to have been with Elijah since Moses was a lad, and he was called Lazarus because, from time to time if he was upset, he would pretend to be dead. Elijah then had to revive him by shouting into his ears or pouring cold water over his nose. To an observer, it appeared that Elijah was miraculously resurrecting Lazarus from the dead.

Lazarus didn't like loud and sudden noises either; on shooting days, the guns had to be kept well away from him while thunderstorms almost made him demented. Man and horse understood each other very well indeed, however, but now it was all over because Elijah had no space to keep a horse at his new cottage. Lazarus had to be sold. I knew Aud Elijah would keep away from the auction at that stage; it would be a sad farewell and he would not wish to see his horse being sold to a stranger. We all hoped that Lazarus would go to a good home, preferably one where he had no need to work. Putting him out to grass seemed a suitable end to his long career.

I did not wait to see the auction of Lazarus because it was my break time. I was quite surprised that Sergeant Blaketon had not driven out to pay me a visit. He loved farm sales and would always find an excuse to rendezvous with his officers when they were on duty. Expecting him to arrive later in the afternoon, I went home, had my lunch and returned to find that further people had arrived. Indeed, a new influx of eager hopefuls was arriving for the afternoon's auction of the furniture and farm equipment. Many of the earlier ones were still in the Hopbind Inn having lunch — some would undoubtedly dwell there for the afternoon — and so I remained on the road to guide in the arriving vehicles. Among the first to return was Aud Elijah.

I wondered who had bought his old horse as I was pondering whether or not I should refer to the matter, he saw me and came across for a chat.

"Things is going very well, Mr Rhea." He nodded across to the barn. "If this afternoon's as good as this morning, I'll not complain."

"There's a good turn-out, Elijah," I commented, noting he had dressed in his best suit. Clearly, he regarded today as a very important occasion and I noted that his grey growth of whiskers had been shaved, his white hair cut and his fingernails cleaned. A sturdy man in his seventies, his face was pink and clear due to the pure moorland air in which he had worked all his life. Everyone liked Aud Elijah.

"Aye, there's a knowledgeable crowd here because I've allus made sure I bought good stuff. Cattle, equipment, stuff for t'house, it's allus been t'best — and folks know that."

"An investment, eh?"

"Aye," he said wistfully. "An investment, it'll keep me and Annie when we get older. Even poor aud Lazarus was an investment, he cost me next to nowt when I bought him, and next to nowt to keep him. It's not oft I've had a vet out to him, he's allus been healthy even when he pretends to be badly. But I shall be able to see him and ride him at his new spot."

"Really?" I was pleased at this news. "Who's bought him?"

"Aud Claude," he smiled. "He'll be as right as rain with Claude."

"Claude Jeremiah Greengrass you mean? What's he want with a horse?" I asked.

"Nay, Mr Rhea, that's summat I can't answer. But Claude says I can pop along there to see t'aud lad and have a ride out from time to time."

We chatted about the sale and his future, then off he went up to the house and into the auctioneer's temporary office to see how things were progressing. I was still puzzling about Claude's purchase as I left my traffic point and went into the barn where the sale of furniture and farm equipment was about to begin. Already, a large crowd had gathered and quite by chance, I discovered Claude admiring a set of dining chairs.

"Mahogany, Mr Rhea," he stroked the splendid polished wood. "Beyond me, though. Some dealer will have an eye on them."

"I'm told you are now the owner of a horse, Claude!" I smiled. "I had no idea you'd come to rescue Lazarus."

"I didn't, Mr Rhea," he said. "Nobody was bidding for him; he's old and past it, you know that as well as me. There was no bids, Mr Rhea, nobody wanted him. They're after prime stock, not summat that's only good for the knacker's yard. Then Rudolph put up the tack; it's about as knackered as the horse that carried it, but I bought yon saddle and stuff because I thought I could sell it on. It's not the quality you'd expect the county set to buy second-hand but it's good enough for me to sell on. So I bid for the tack and got a fair saddle, bridle and so on. The snag was, Mr Rhea, I got the horse an' all. I hadn't caught Rudolph's words, you see, I had no idea he was giving the tack away with the horse, or the horse with the tack, depending how you look at it. I just wanted the tack, I got the lot for a tenner. Horse and tack."

"*Caveat emptor*," I smiled at him.

"Eh?"

"Buyer beware, Claude. It means it's a binding deal; you should have been certain what you were bidding for."

"Aye, well, Aud Elijah can come and ride his horse whenever he wants. I've told him that. I've a stable and mebbe I can use Lazarus for hacking or summat. That'll earn his keep."

"Well, be careful if you make another bid!"

"I will, 'cos there's a trunk. I've my eye on. I've looked at it, mind, it's full of old clothes and things . . ." And he tapped the side of his nose to indicate I should not tell anyone of his intention. I would not — and we parted. Afterwards, I learned that Claude had indeed succeeded in his bid to buy the old wooden trunk of clothes and it now awaited collection by him. Lazarus was also waiting patiently in his stable for Claude to take him to his new home, but Claude had gone to the Hopbind Inn for a celebratory drink. Whatever was in that trunk had pleased him greatly and he had felt the urge to share his delight with his pals. He was still there when the auction ended.

I waited around the premises as the buyers paid their bills and collected their newly acquired goods and chattels, then went down to the gate to guide the outgoing cars, cattle trucks and vans on to the road. A steady stream of traffic was soon departing without causing me any real problems when I noticed Claude Jeremiah Greengrass heading down the farm track towards me. He was leading Lazarus with a short rein and was talking to the horse; strapped on to the saddle was his recently acquired trunk. Somehow, he had balanced it on the horse's back and it was held in place with straps and ropes as Lazarus bore it down the lane. He looked like a pack horse of old as he bore the ungainly load towards me. The first thing that impressed me was that the trunk looked unsafe on the horse's back; even as I watched, it had moved slightly and was tending to hang down at one side. The web of straps and ropes appeared to be holding it, however, and Claude continued towards me, walking Lazarus on the grass beside the track to allow the outgoing vehicles to pass. Lazarus did not appear at all bothered about the proximity or the noise of the traffic and seemed happy to follow his new lord and master. So far, the horse had not gone to sleep which meant he was quite content.

"So you got the trunk, Claude?" I greeted him as he reached my point.

"Aye, Mr Rhea, *caveat emptor* and all that. I got just what I wanted today, more than I wanted really. Do you want to buy a good aud gallower?"

I thought his voice sounded rather slurred; I would not have said he was drunk but without doubt he had been imbibing in the Hopbind Inn and had consumed more than normal, especially at this time of day. In my opinion, he was not sufficiently under the influence of his drinking to be unfit to be in charge of the horse. Tiddly perhaps, but not drunk.

"No thanks, Claude, I have no wish to buy a horse. Now, is that trunk safe on his back?"

"Safe as houses, Mr Rhea," he said. "I lashed it on myself, reef knots galore, and a few round turns, half hitches, timber hitches and clove hitches."

"I hope you get it home without a hitch," I grinned.

"Lazarus knows his job, Mr Rhea, he's not likely to break into a gallop or even a trot, not in his state. I just hope he gets home without dropping dead."

"Or pretending to be dead?" I reminded Claude of Lazarus's propensity for feigning death when he was upset.

And so man, horse and wobbly trunk emerged from the farm track and turned towards Elsinby. Claude had a long walk back to his ranch and I guessed he would be completely sober by the time he arrived. Reflecting upon the events of that day, I felt it had all proceeded very smoothly — but I had not bargained for Sergeant Blaketon's impending arrival.

As the procession of vehicles was leaving Skeugh Heights, with most of them turning towards Elsinby, Sergeant Blaketon was heading in the opposite direction with the intention of paying me a supervisory visit. He was driving his official black Ford Anglia which, as usual, was as clean as the proverbial new pin with its paintwork, glass and chrome parts gleaming in the setting sun.

Although I did not witness the incident which followed, I learned the details from motorists who had been near the scene, and of course, I had to cope with both Greengrass and Blaketon, to say nothing of Lazarus.

Because most of the sale traffic, by this stage travelling in a continuous procession, was heading towards Elsinby on the left of that rural road, Claude decided to walk Lazarus in the same direction, but on the right of the highway. In these particular circumstances, it was a logical thing to do even though the Highway Code recommended riding horses on the left. For one thing, Claude was then facing any oncoming traffic and for another, the busy traffic could flow smoothly along that narrow road.

Sergeant Blaketon was heading in the opposite direction in his shining official police car. Narrow though the road was, there was adequate room for the sergeant's small vehicle — until he was confronted by Greengrass leading a horse which was carrying a large trunk. Knowing how Claude's mind functioned, I could guess his behaviour — he would force Blaketon to a halt and then refuse to budge, thus blocking the sergeant's route. Indeed, this is what happened.

"Greengrass, get that old nag out of my way! I want to get past!" the sergeant had shouted from his driver's window.

"Lazarus has as much right on the highway as you, Sergeant!" Claude had chuckled. "You are causing the obstruction, not him! You back up, there's a gateway half a mile up the road!"

As this banter was in progress, cars, vans and cattle trucks leaving Skeugh Heights were chugging past in a continuous procession, oblivious of the drama being played nearby.

Blaketon was getting angrier by this stage and bellowed, "Now look, I am not reversing halfway back to Elsinby just for an old horse and an old rogue. You back away, you can turn that animal around and get into a field or somewhere till I get past."

"Why should I?" was Claude's response. "I was here first!"

The argument soon developed into a loud and vociferous slanging match with neither protagonist giving way, until Sergeant Blaketon had had enough. He slammed his fist on to the car horn and blasted it as loudly as he could. The effect was dramatic. Lazarus reared in terror, standing on his hind legs and whinnying loudly as the noise alarmed him but in standing on his rear legs, the old trunk slid from its moorings on his back and crashed on to the road surface. It was clearly in a fragile condition because it burst open to spill a selection of old clothes on to the road — and the terrified horse, moving around in its fright, trod on some of the clothes. There was a tremendous explosion — and Lazarus collapsed to the ground, narrowly missing two cars but effectively blocking the road.

"What in the name of . . ." Blaketon climbed out to survey the damage. All traffic had to halt while Claude, his eyes wide with surprise, surveyed the wreckage of his trunk. Gingerly, he stooped down and recovered a shotgun which had been hidden among the clothing — it was a beauty . . . but it had been loaded and Lazarus's actions had released both barrels.

Happily, the shot had whizzed harmlessly through the hedge.

"Greengrass! Has your horse been shot?"

"No, Sergeant, he always pretends to be dead when he's upset or frightened."

"Well, he can't lie there all day holding up the traffic. He's not the only one who's upset and frightened! That gun, Greengrass! It was loaded — and I suspect you are drunk. You are drunk in charge of a loaded firearm and you are drunk in charge of a horse . . . I'll have you for this, Greengrass."

"I knew the gun was there, that's why I bought the trunk, I don't want those old clothes, but I had no idea the thing was loaded . . . anyway, look at my horse, Sergeant, he's dead!"

It was while this kerfuffle was under way that I was called to the scene and arrived to find what appeared to be a dead horse in the middle of a traffic jam, with Sergeant Blaketon and Greengrass enjoying a real ding-dong among it all. After being informed of the events which had led to this confrontation, I managed to calm them down but my first priority was to move Lazarus so that traffic could flow again.

"Elijah knows how to revive him," I said to Claude. "Didn't he tell you?"

"Aye, but it doesn't work, Mr Rhea. I've blown up his nose and shouted into his ears, but he hasn't moved. And I haven't any water to chuck over him, not here."

"He's clearly very upset!" grunted Blaketon. "I'm not surprised, anybody who has nearly been shot would be upset."

"We'll have to get Elijah to revive him," I said.

I persuaded Sergeant Blaketon to call Ashfordly Police Station on his car radio with a request that Alf Ventress, the duty constable, ring Skeugh Heights to ask Elijah to come quickly. He was there within minutes, looking down at his old horse. In the meantime, a small crowd had gathered to see what the problem was.

"Lazarus you bloody nitwit!" Elijah shouted, kneeling close to the horse's head. "You can't play dead in the middle of a road like this . . . come on, you daft old bugger, don't take the huff, I'll see you again soon." And he shouted into the ears of the inert horse.

But there was no reaction from Lazarus.

"You've really upset him!" snapped Claude at Blaketon. "I've never known a man upset a horse as much as you have."

"Greengrass, you are drunk and you are liable to be arrested if you don't shut up. Besides, it was your shotgun, your loaded shotgun, that frightened him, not me."

"It was you blasting that horn that upset him, not me. Anyroad, I didn't know it was loaded. Who'd be daft enough to store a loaded gun among clothes?"

I left them to their arguing as I stooped beside the still horse. Elijah was still attempting to revive him, hoping to perform his noted "back to life" routine. But it wasn't working this time.

"I think he really is dead, Mr Rhea," he said at length, looking into my face with misty eyes.

"The shots didn't hit him, did they?" I could see no sign of injury on the horse.

"Nay, it's just that he got his time over," said Elijah. "Mebbe he couldn't live without me, eh?"

"You could be right. I'd better get a vet," I said. I asked among the motorists if there was a veterinary surgeon among them, and there was one in the traffic queue, right at the back and well beyond the range of this incident. Someone ran to fetch him. A smiling man in his fifties, he came forward at my request and examined Lazarus.

"I've known him for years, this old horse. I never imagined you'd sell him, Elijah." He stroked the still face and caressed his ears. "Playing dead has been his party trick for as long as I can remember, but he's not playing now, Elijah. He's gone, his heart has stopped. There's no sign of life. I shall certify him dead."

"I paid good money for him," Claude began.

"Shut up, Claude!" I snapped at him, seeing tears rolling down the cheeks of poor old Elijah. "You bought a saddle, and got the horse for nowt. You've still got the saddle."

"Poor aud lad." Elijah was standing beside his old friend, repeating those words over and over again as I sent for a tractor and trailer to remove the corpse. Claude had sobered up by this time, and Blaketon had calmed down. By the time we cleared away the mortal remains of dear old Lazarus, traffic was flowing, good humour had returned and Claude had accepted the situation. His purchase of the old trunk had been his reason for attending the sale, knowing of the valuable old gun which was hidden inside, and he was content.

Someone offered him a lift home, along with his tack, trunk and gun, and he accepted before Blaketon tackled him again about his inebriation. He allowed Elijah to take the remains of Lazarus away for burial — there was no way Elijah would allow a knacker's yard to have the remains. He would bury Lazarus in the garden of his new cottage.

"I don't think we can proceed against Claude," I said to Sergeant Blaketon when the traffic was moving and the queues had faded away. "He wasn't really drunk, just a bit tipsy. He was sober enough when it was all over."

"I wonder if he has a gun licence for that weapon?" mused Blaketon. "I might just pop in tomorrow to ask him . . ."

I groaned, but Sergeant Blaketon drove off with a smile on his face.

That night, I sat before my fire with a novel, thinking over the day's events. Had anyone been the loser? I wondered. Claude had got his gun and a saddle he could sell, and he had never wanted to buy Lazarus anyway. And Elijah had got him back — even if the old horse was dead.

Then my telephone rang. It was Elijah.

"You'll never guess what's happened, Mr Rhea." He sounded very happy.

"No, what's happened, Elijah?" I asked.

"Lazarus. I went out to wash him down and when I put the cold water on his nose, he came round, as large as life. Back from the dead again, Mr Rhea. By, he is a real sod, is aud Lazarus! You can never tell where you are with him!"

"I'm delighted, Elijah, I really am," I said with feeling. "I know how much you thought of him."

"But is he my horse now, Mr Rhea, that's what I want to know? That's why I'm ringing you this late. I mean, I did put the poor aud chap up for sale and Claude did buy him . . ."

"Claude bought a saddle and some other tack," I said. "He had no idea he was getting Lazarus as well. But you'd best have words with him tomorrow, eh?"

And he rang off, a happy man.

I went straight round to visit Claude, wanting to prevent any trouble he might cause with poor old Elijah over the ownership of Lazarus.

"But that's my horse, Mr Rhea, I paid good money for him!" he protested.

"No, Claude, you bid for a saddle and tack, which is what you got. Might I suggest you let Elijah keep the horse — and maybe, because he has nowhere to keep Lazarus when he moves into his cottage, you could rent him grazing on your premises . . . that way, you'd earn a bob or two without the expense of keeping the horse."

"I'll have to think about it, Mr Rhea," he muttered, and from the tone of his voice and the gleam in his eye, I felt he was already dreaming up some devious scheme. I felt he would put pressure on Elijah to return the horse to the official new owner.

"Well, Claude," I smiled. "While you are thinking about it, I might be thinking about asking if you have a licence for the gun you bought at auction, and I might be considering submitting a report about you being drunk in charge of a loaded firearm, and drunk in charge of a horse . . ."

"Mebbe Elijah could keep Lazarus, eh?" he grunted.

"It's up to you, Claude," I said as I walked out of his house.

8. GREENGRASS IN BUSINESS

You do not even know your own foolish business.
   THE EARL OF CHESTERFIELD, 1694–1773

One of the prevailing problems for police officers, which seemed particularly prevalent in the 1960s, was the dishonest person who failed to settle his or her household debts, or the crooked businessman or woman who produced inferior services or products and then passed them off as works of quality. Simple examples include those who do not pay their bills at the local shop or garage, and those who perform third-rate work which is later discovered to be defective, usually after payment has been made.

One very common occurrence in the 1960s was work performed by what became known as the Leeds Gangs because it was rogues from Leeds who started the trick. A number of men, usually two or three, would arrive at a house which was occupied by an elderly but well-off person. They would point out that while driving past, they had "happened" to notice that the chimney stack appeared to be faulty or that the roof looked as if it was in a dangerous condition or even that a tile was missing or broken. Most generously, and even in a friendly manner, they would offer to inspect the roof or chimney in question at close quarters, but would then terrify the householder into thinking the entire roof or chimney was in imminent danger of collapse, or that the leaking roof would produce colossal rain damage unless it was repaired immediately.

Having alarmed the householder, the next step was to offer to repair the damage — with a substantial sum of cash in advance "for materials" — and when the task was done, an inflated cash payment was demanded for the work. The work was invariably of poor quality or even totally unnecessary and some of the gangs simply took the cash given to them to "buy the materials", and never returned.

A similar trick operates in the 1990s with groups of men offering to resurface private household drives with tarmacadam. An inflated cash payment is demanded, and the work is either unnecessary or of abysmally low standard. Because there is no criminal deception, the police are powerless to prevent these abuses. The borderline between such practices and criminal offences has always been very blurred indeed, and the operators manage to stay on the right side of the law — but only just!

The problem is that the victims often approach the police for help in such cases, usually in the belief they have redress through criminal law. The sad truth is that a high proportion of such matters are of no concern to the police because they are civil disputes. At times, it can be very difficult explaining this to an aggrieved person who may feel that the police don't care and that they are not interested in their problems. The truth is that little or nothing can be done by the police if no crime has been committed. A crime is not the same thing as a civil wrong.

An added problem is that retribution through the civil courts is difficult and sometimes enormously expensive, even if it were possible to produce a case against the perpetrators. After all, who is to judge whether work is poor? The workman would surely insist it was up to standard and if a price was agreed before the work was done, it is very difficult to win redress from any source.

With a man like Claude Jeremiah Greengrass operating on my beat at Aidensfield, it is fair to say that I received many calls from a host of highly dissatisfied customers but there was little one could do — officially — to rectify the matter. Most of his business transactions were unsatisfactory indeed and although I did threaten him with action in the criminal courts if any of his dodgy activities justified my intervention, he continued to behave in a very dubious manner. One example was his holy-water enterprise.

On one of my routine patrols during a bright spring morning, I wanted to ask if he had been offered any cigarettes or bottles of whisky which had been stolen from the Co-op at Strensford. I arrived to find him working in an outbuilding. With a battered old watering can and a funnel, he was filling dozens of empty sauce bottles which stood on a table before him. Alfred, his faithful dog, was lying at his feet but slunk away as I approached.

"Now, Claude," I said as I walked into the dark shed, "stocking up with water, are we? Do you know something, I don't? Is there a drought on the way?"

"It's nowt to do with the law what I sell, Constable!" he said. "It's a new business I'm setting up. All above board. Legal and that."

"It's not gin, is it?" I laughed. "It looks like water to me."

"It is water," he chuckled. "Pure, moorland water."

"And you're going to sell it?" I felt I was missing something important because I could not imagine sane Yorkshire folk spending their hard-earned brass on bottles of moorland water when bucket-loads could be obtained quite free of charge with a modicum of effort.

"It's from that well in Harland's Intake," he said. "I bought the intake, which means the water that flows there is mine." Intake was the name given to an area of moorland which had been enclosed many years earlier; a dry-stone wall had been constructed around the moorland in question to form a small paddock. Such intakes were invariably named after the person who first enclosed them. Harland's Intake lay above Aidensfield on the edge of the moors and Claude used it for grazing some of his sheep.

"So what's special about this water?" I knew he was waiting for me to ask the question. "Folks will only buy it if there's something very special about it."

"There's a spring in the corner of the intake," Claude grinned. "Alfred was digging for rabbits there one day and uncovered it. There was this lovely flow of water trickling from underground, fresh and tasty as wine, it is. It bubbles up in one spot, runs a few yards down my land in a natural drain, then vanishes underground again. Wasted really. Now I happened to be talking to a chap who knows this part of the world like the back of his hand, and he said it was St Aiden's Well."

"Really? Can that be verified?"

"Oh, aye," Claude beamed, with a look of satisfaction on his face. "Just you take a look at that old book over there."

As he continued to fill the bottles, I located a battered old leather-bound book on a shelf. It was open at a page which described the well. There was even a line drawing of St Aiden's Well, and a map showing its location. According to local legend, St Aiden had been engaged on missionary work in this area around AD 643 and had established a short-term camp-site on the moor. He had chosen the area now occupied by Claude's intake because of the never-ending supply of fresh, pure water from a moorland spring. Thus the spring had become known as St Aiden's Well. It had been regarded as a holy well because the water was so pure and health-giving that it was said to effect remarkable cures. Normal water in those times was foul and polluted; it caused terrible disease and plagues. Pure water did not actually cure people, it merely failed to make them ill, and so the people thought it was miraculous.

For many years, St Aiden's Well had been a shrine with pilgrims trekking from far and wide to sample the goodness from its waters. During the Reformation, the well had been covered up and pilgrims were fined if they came to pray here

— the new Protestant faith did not like overtly religious fervour and sometimes confused it with superstition. Now, it seemed, the rabbit-digging Alfred had rediscovered the holy well. And Claude intended to cash in upon his good fortune.

"It's holy water, you see, Constable, and there's a big demand for the stuff. This could be the next Lourdes. It could become a place of pilgrimage; folks from all over the world could be coming to Aidensfield to take the waters."

I could hardly anticipate Harland's Intake becoming as busy as Lourdes, and so I said, "Claude, that's not holy water. It's a moorland spring, nothing more."

"It's been blessed by St Aiden, Constable!"

"I very much doubt it. Besides, he came here thirteen hundred years ago; the water he blessed wouldn't have hung around all this time. The water you're bottling has been flavoured by hundreds of generations of moorland sheep, not blessed by a good and holy saint," I added.

"I hope you're not going to spread doubts about the quality of my water!" he grumbled.

"Would you drink it?" I put to him.

"That's nowt to do with this. This is a businessman's dream — you get your ingredients for nowt, you scrounge empty bottles from the hotels and chip shops, and you take time filling 'em with pure water. Then you sell 'em. It's all profit, Constable, there's no outlay. Well, except for getting the labels printed, they'll be ready tomorrow. That's what I call a bloody good business!"

"In other words, you wouldn't risk drinking this water?"

He blinked furiously, trying to avoid my gaze as he countered with, "If it's good enough for Alfred to drink, it's good enough for folks to buy!"

"There will be folks who are daft enough to buy your water, Claude and if they do, you deserve some credit." I then turned to the real reason for my presence. Claude could offer no help on the Co-op raid and I left him as he emerged from the shed to refill his watering can from St Aiden's Well on the moor above his home.

A couple of days later I was in Joe Steel's shop in Aidensfield. He was serving Miss Wynn who lived in Lingside Cottage on the outskirts of the village and, as I awaited my turn, I noticed on one side of the counter, a row of six former sauce bottles bearing smart new labels on white paper with dark blue printing. I picked one up for a closer look. Each was filled with a clear liquid and labelled *Holy Water — Fresh from St Aiden's Well. 2s. 6d.*

Underneath in smaller print, was the wording. *Pilgrimmes from farre and wyde came to drynk ye water as a miraculous cure for all pestilences, plagues, maladies and diseases. Ye ancient holy well, newly discovered in ye most secret of locations, is flowing again after 1300 years with 50,000 gallons ye day of ye holiest of water this side of Lourdes. Amen.*

"Joe," I addressed the shopkeeper when my turn came. "You haven't bought this stuff from Claude, have you?"

"Bought it? Not likely. But I said he could put some here for sale if he wanted, with a bit of commission for me if any are sold, that's if anybody's daft enough to buy water from Claude's intake. He seems to think tourists will flock to drink it."

Even as I spoke, I noticed Miss Wynn pick up a bottle as she was leaving the shop. After examining the label, she placed half-a-crown in payment on the counter and shouted her thanks to Joe. The astonishing thing was that another five people did buy Claude's holy water. Every bottle had gone by closing time. The following day Joe told me that they had all been snapped up by villagers and that he had ordered more stocks. And one of the buyers was Dr Alex Ferguson's receptionist!

I discovered this when I called on the doctor. As I entered the surgery, I noticed Miss Wynn, her skin a peculiar shade of green, waiting for the doctor to examine her. Coming into the waiting room to call in the next patient, Dr Ferguson noticed my arrival — he knew I had come to ask about the progress of a statement he was making about the casualty of a recent road accident. The accident had occurred the previous week and the casualty had complained of suffering from shock, a condition later diagnosed by Dr Ferguson and I needed a statement to that effect from the doctor who had attended the scene. Happily, it had been prepared and was awaiting my arrival.

"I'm sorry for the delay, Nick," smiled Alex Ferguson, handing me the envelope. "But my receptionist is ill, she's not been in today. Tummy trouble. There's a lot of it about, a bug going round the village, I think."

"You as well, Miss Wynn?" I asked, thinking her face looked like a dollop of green chewing gum.

"Yes, I'm afraid so . . . I do need something for my stomach, Doctor." She arose to follow him into the surgery.

As she was walking towards the surgery door, I joked, "You need some of that holy water of Claude's, he reckons it's a miracle cure for almost anything!"

"I do not!" she snapped. "That's what made me ill! And Mrs Lucas down the road . . . poor old thing, she's been sat on the toilet ever since six o'clock this morning."

Dr Ferguson halted in his doorway and turned to face us. "What's all this about?" he asked.

I explained about Claude's new enterprise and Miss Wynn confirmed she had bought one of the bottles, drinking half its contents before going to bed last night. During the night she had experienced the most awful stomach pains, followed by nausea, vomiting and diarrhoea. Dr Ferguson listened and nodded, saying he'd had other patients in this morning, all with the same symptoms.

"I think St Aiden's Well needs to be examined by a holy-water expert!" I laughed.

"And I think Claude Jeremiah Greengrass should be made to drink a gallon of the stuff!" grunted the doctor. "Come in, Miss Wynn, let's see if we can find something to settle your stomach." I went straight over to Joe's shop and suggested he withdraw the water from sale, whereupon he said that a further ten people had bought supplies. Six were from Aidensfield, but the others were holidaymakers in a car passing through. He had no idea who they were, but would take it from his shelves until he had had some proof from Claude that his water was not contaminated. Claude had been producing more bottles than were on sale in Aidensfield — according to Joe, he'd taken supplies to Elsinby, Ashfordly, Ploatby and several other villages with stores and post offices. In the meantime, Joe said he would ensure he had plenty of toilet rolls and stomach powders on sale.

I thought I had better warn Claude not to offer any more of his miracle water for sale and drove my minivan out to his ranch. He was not in, however. The doors were locked and there was no sign of Alfred either. I would return later. As I was leaving a local farmer called Sam Lester was heading towards me on his tractor. He halted, climbed down and came to speak to me.

"Is he in?" were Sam's first words. Sam was a man in his early fifties who always wore a flat cap over his lank fair hair, and who always appeared in need of a shave. He was scruffily dressed in his working clothes and a black and white Border collie accompanied him. Sam worked Swinney Top Farm on the moors above Aidensfield, his house enjoying one of the most spectacular views in Yorkshire. He specialised in black-faced sheep and Highland cattle.

"No, he's out," I said. "I'll come back."

"Will he be in the pub tonight?" Sam asked, as if I knew every one of Claude's movements.

"No idea, Sam, but that's where he usually gets to. Can I give him a message if I see him?"

"Has your missus bought any of that holy water of his?" was Sam's next blunt question.

"I hope not," I informed him. "It seems to be making everybody sick."

"It's put our Cynthia on the bog for most of today!" he snapped. "Running and shouting about the house, she is, when there's work to be done. Just wait till I get my hands on Greengrass! Holy water my foot! It's liquid manure he's selling!"

"Don't take the law into your own hands, Sam," I warned him, as he stomped away. Moments later, he was returning along his route and I was following, wondering how many other people had gone down with Claude's syndrome.

I failed to locate Claude that afternoon; he had not been seen around Aidensfield and I began to wonder if he had fled the country. Dr Ferguson was seeking him too, hoping to persuade him to withdraw his water before the authorities decided to test it, but Claude had vanished. He turned up in the pub that evening and I happened to be in; I was off duty and had popped in for a quiet pint or two, arriving an hour or so before Claude, but the night promised to be anything other than relaxed with Claude Jeremiah Greengrass in the bar. It seemed he had gone over the moors to Pickering to conclude a deal for a house clearance, and so he had missed all the fuss about the effect of his holy water.

In his absence, however, the locals, with George's cooperation, had concocted some kind of plot against him, knowing he would come into the bar that evening, and the details had been finalised before my and Claude's arrival. I was asked not to mention holy water if Claude came in, so I had no idea what was going on. The ringleader was Sam Lester and there were others with him who did not usually drink this early.

As the evening progressed, however, their plot was revealed. From his jacket pocket, the now smartly dressed Sam produced a bottle of the size that contained medicine from the doctor and showed it to his pals. It was full of water and bore a smart label saying, *St Cuthbert's Mineral Water. 2s. Pure water from St Cuthbert's ancient well.*

"This is cheaper than yours, Claude!" grinned Sam. "My wife saw yours, then I saw this for sale in Ashfordly and reckoned it's a better bargain."

Claude grabbed the bottle and examined it.

"It's a smaller bottle, so it should cost less, besides, where's this St Cuthbert's Well?" he asked Sam.

"I've no idea, but this is better tasting than yours, Claude. There's a slight hint of lemon with just a touch of ling and blackberry flavour, and it includes a slight fizz when it's opened. And it's not smaller than yours, it's just a different shaped bottle. Good value for money, I reckon. I thought I'd show this bottle to George, in case he wants to stock it and sell it here. Then mebbe Joe in the shop will stock it."

"He stocks mine, he can't sell inferior stuff!"

"Well, he reckons this is better than yours, Claude. Want to taste some for yourself?"

Claude blinked furiously as he was placed in this compromising position, but he dare not admit he had never tasted his own product. He took the bottle, opened it and sniffed. His nose wrinkled as he attempted to define the flavours mentioned by Sam, and then he took a sip.

"You need a good swig," said Sam. "To get the proper effect, that is."

"Aye," said another man. "A real good sip . . . now my wife's got some of your water, Claude, so maybe this'll persuade her to change to Cuthbert's."

Claude had drunk well over half a bottle of the new potion without commenting on its bouquet or taste and we all watched with deepening interest.

"So," asked Sam eventually, as Claude paused.

"I must admit this tastes good," Claude said. "I can taste liquorice in this one, I think, or summat strong and good for the body . . ." and he drank more. The men smiled knowingly as he sampled the water.

"Do you reckon folks'll stick with my holy water?" asked Claude, having drained the bottle. "I mean, this is good stuff, but not a patch on mine . . . if I bring my prices down, they might stay with mine. Quality allus tells in the long run."

"I should get your trousers down and prepare for a lot of short runs," grinned Sam. "That is your water, Claude." And he proceeded to explain what had happened to others who had consumed far less than Claude. They'd all had the runs.

Claude looked at the bottle . . .

"You can't do this to me . . ."

And then Dr Ferguson came into the bar.

"Claude Greengrass!" he boomed. "I've been looking for you all day. Do you realise that dozens of my patients have been condemned to a day on the toilet because of your holy water? Now, listen to me, either you withdraw that stuff or else I get the authorities to test it, and you could get fined or sued or something for the trouble you have caused."

Claude's face was a picture now.

"How long's it take to work?" he asked Sam.

"Just time for you to get home and get established on the bog, and with all that water inside you, you'll be there all night and all day tomorrow . . . and if you sell that miserable stuff again, I'll have your guts for garters!"

And with that warning lingering in his ears, Claude clutched his stomach and ran from the pub.

"What's matter with him?" smiled Dr Ferguson, after ordering a whisky.

"He's had a taste of his own medicine," grinned George from behind the bar.

* * *

Another of Claude's trouble-spots was his chimney sweeping enterprise. From time to time, armed with his sooty collection of bags and brushes, he could be seen trudging around Aidensfield as he tried to win custom from wary villagers, but those of long standing in the community knew better than to employ him. After hearing about or experiencing his clumsy attempts to rid their chimneys of soot and other deposits, they preferred the services of professionals from Ashfordly or Strensford. Claude's reputation for leaving more mess than there was when he started his work, resulted in him rarely finding that kind of employment.

Newcomers, however, were never party to such well-kept secrets. If they saw a notice in the shop window saying, *Chimney Sweeping. Local Contractor. Renowned for clean, tidy and swift Work. Reasonable rates. Contact C.J. Greengrass*, then they would apply and he would turn up with his equipment. As a rule, such people never employed him again. Indeed, it has been said that the effect of Claude upon their new life drove them back from whence they came.

The problem with newcomers was that they were often dewy-eyed townies with impracticable expectations of country life. Blissfully unaware of the harsh realities of living on the moors, they bought rundown cottages that no wise rustic would even contemplate living in even if they were modernised and restored. Many of these incomers spent their weekends sitting before log fires as they listened for the sound of the curlew or the cuckoo. It generally required only one blizzard-ridden, freezing winter to persuade them that it wasn't heaven after all.

The snag with log fires is that they soon clog up the chimneys with their carbonised deposits and while the swiftest and most effective means of clearing the grime is a roaring chimney fire, such a method can set the entire house alight — along with any neighbouring properties. Such a fierce inferno will surely attract the interest of passers-by who immediately summon the fire brigade. A really good chimney fire in full throttle sounds like the roar of Victoria Falls, and tongues of fire will shoot from the top to emulate the finest of flame throwers. However efficient they may be, they are not recommended for cleaning chimneys.

In fact, chimney fires were unlawful by virtue of the Town Police Clauses Act of 1847, which was still effective in urban areas when I was a serving constable. A person who allowed a chimney to catch fire could be fined ten shillings (50p). It was a defence to claim that the fire was not due to any omission, neglect or carelessness and if the court believed that, it could result in a not guilty decision. Generally, it was reckoned if a chimney did catch fire, it must have been due to some carelessness, such as allowing too much soot or excessive deposits to accumulate through a lack of regular chimney clearing.

I must admit that Claude did not use such drastic measures, even on the most difficult of smoke-stacks. From time to time, though, he did use one traditional method — if his brushes failed to dislodge a stubborn mass, he would pack the fireplace with holly twigs and set fire to them. The up-draught would carry the blazing holly into the chimney to dislodge a substantial amount of soot and loosen the rest. The loose soot would fall into the hearth where it could be collected.

In addition to these methods, Claude had his own bizarre way of coping with the many troublesome flues in and around Aidensfield. Because most of his commissions entailed him working on older properties, and because he lacked modern sophisticated suction equipment, his unique method was often required. As these properties were often occupied by weekenders or rented as holiday cottages, word of Claude's methods seldom passed from one hapless visitor to another. The people who bought these old houses were often dreamers but I think it is fair to say that Claude gave them a nightmare vision of rural life — this was especially so in the case of the Mr and Mrs Crowberry of Rigg Side Cottage, a lonely hovel on the hills between Aidensfield and Ashfordly.

Amelia Crowberry, née Leatherleigh came from a wealthy family and existed on an allowance from daddy; she had met and married a weird youth called Abraham Crowberry whom the police would describe, without any hint of political incorrectness, as a layabout. Amelia, well into her mid-thirties, slightly overweight and wearing little rounded spectacles, kept him in the manner to which she felt he ought to be accustomed which meant she did everything for him.

She paid with daddy's generous allowance. Abraham never did a stroke of work, sometimes sitting and thinking all day and sometimes just sitting. I was never sure whether daddy had ever met Abraham but in the circumstances, I felt he hadn't; no self-respecting dad would encourage his offspring to mate with and maintain such a useless specimen of the male human animal.

Wanting to commune with nature and having a massive desire to save the planet from people like huntsmen, fishermen, rabbit-catchers and whalers, the happy couple bought Rigg Side Cottage from a local farmer. They made the shack habitable, reroofed it and installed a flushing toilet, hot and cold water and electricity, then spent their days playing flutes and worrying about the effects of pollution, the cruelty of nature, nuclear reactors, the under-privileged in Liverpool and whether flowers held the secret of eternal life. And they burnt lots and lots of logs on their open fire.

It didn't take long for their living room chimney to become clogged with the deposits of burnt birch, beech and blackthorn, not to mention conifer wood, hawthorn and sycamore and all the other timbers they collected from the local woodlands. In need of a clean sweep, they contacted the local expert — Claude Jeremiah Greengrass. After assuring themselves that he used only traditional methods without resorting to any fearsome, atmosphere-polluting or planet-destroying chemicals, he was hired.

An account of what followed was told to me by Amelia when she came to complain about Claude's methods.

In his old truck, Claude had arrived at Rigg Side Cottage complete with chimney brushes, protective cloths and Alfred, his dog. After consuming several cups of a brownish-coloured liquid prepared by Amelia (Abraham lay on the settee to consume his), Claude had reaffirmed his expertise in coping with rural chimneys and advised Amelia to cover everything in the living room.

Abraham was compelled to move his twenty-seven-year-old carcass while Amelia in her loose, overflowing purple dress, had draped their sparse furnishings with old sheets. Meanwhile, Claude had positioned in front of the open fireplace, a soot-stained drape with a hole in the middle. His round-headed black brush with one section of its handle attached, was already in position with the handle protruding through the hole. Claude had next secured the cloth to the mantelpiece and floor with bricks, the idea being that no soot would escape into the room.

Thrusting the head of the brush up the chimney, he had attached further lengths of handle which forced the brush head higher into the great black void beyond. Even at that stage, heavy deposits were crashing into the fireplace behind the cloth. So far, there was no problem, things appeared to be progressing very satisfactorily. Amelia had remained in the living room, Abraham having settled in the adjoining room which, it seemed, he used as a study. It was full of his paintings of wild flowers, which, to the unskilled eye, looked more like the paint-scattering activities of a three-year-old child. It seemed that Abraham hoped, one day, to sell a few of these but in the meantime was lying on an old couch, semi-comatose, dreaming about a society where nothing was killed or destroyed.

"It's stuck," Claude had said to Amelia as he had heaved at the brush. "There's an obstruction up there, my brushes won't go any higher."

"Oh dear," Amelia had simpered. "Does that mean you can't complete the job?"

"Complete the job? No job is too tough for the chimney sweeping champion of Aidensfield, Mrs Crowberry. Now, it just means a bit more planning."

He went outside to examine the structure of the chimney line which ascended the outer wall of the cottage. Amelia was with him and Claude, the expert that he was, had revealed the structure which contained her chimneys. It was shaped like a letter A without the crosspiece, the chimneys from the living room and Abraham's study rising against the outside wall to come together in a single chimney stack. There were two separate chimney pots, however, so each chimney was independent of the other, but the snag was that neither chimney rose smoothly — each side of the giant A was zigzagged and each rose in a series of small steps to the stack on top. The alignment of those steps was enough to frustrate the through-passage of a chimneysweep's brush and the interior of each would be like miniature staircases with huge deposits of soot upon each step — all beyond the reach of Claude's brushes.

"So if the chimneys are a series of steps," simpered Amelia, "it means your brushes can't get through? You can't reach all that soot that's collected there!"

"Greengrass never fails," Claude had beamed. "I have a second line of attack that is guaranteed. Now, have you a ladder?"

There's one in the outbuildings," she had said.

"Right, when I give you the word, you go indoors and take my Alfred with you. Place him at the bottom of the chimney, near the brush handles that are there. He'll know what to do when I shout to him. He'll hear my voice coming down the chimney."

Having positioned the ladder so that he could reach the chimney pots from the outside of the house, Claude had sent Amelia indoors accompanied by Alfred and then went to his old van for a sack; it contained a living thing. A hen, in fact. Clutching the sack, Claude had ascended the ladder, opened the sack and lifted out a large white hen which cackled a lot and flapped its wings.

"Ready, Mrs Crowberry?" he shouted down the chimney.

"Yes," came the faint voice from below.

"Right, action stations." And he had thrust the protesting hen down the chimney from the top, shouting at it as it descended, its flapping wings dislodging thick deposits of soot which fell into the depths. The tiny steps were too narrow for the bird to gain a perch; besides, it was pitch black inside and it had no idea where to put its feet.

"Alfred!" shouted Claude, whereupon Alfred began to bark below. His high-pitched woofing echoed up the chimney as the terrified hen had bounced up and down on frantically flapping wings, flying in alarm from one dark corner to the next, as it dislodged an enormous amount of deposited soot. With Claude bellowing from above and Alfred barking from below, the hen had continued to flap up and down until it seemed that most of the soot had been dislodged. It now lay in a deep pile behind Claude's safety drape.

Claude had descended the ladder and entered the living room to find a puzzled Mrs Crowberry and Alfred who was wagging his tail; Alfred found his part in Claude's chimney sweeping quite exciting.

"Mr Greengrass," said Amelia quite angrily, "was that a live bird you caused to enter my chimney?"

"Aye, Clara Cluck, my old hen, she loves it. Team work it is, you see, me, Alfred and Clara. No job too difficult, no job left unfinished! That's our slogan."

"Mr Greengrass, I think that is disgraceful; it is cruelty. I have a good mind to report you to the RSPCA and to the police, for cruelty to a hen."

"It's not cruel, she loves it! It would be cruel if the fire was on, but it's not. You'll see, when I remove that drape, she'll come out of there bright-eyed and ready for another go. She'll be there waiting; she knows her job, does Clara. She's the finest chimney sweeping hen this side of the Pennines."

Not convinced, Mrs Crowberry had stood with her arms folded as Claude began to remove the drape; Alfred was waiting too, tail wagging and anxious to share their joy at the return of Clara Cluck.

"The trick is to catch her before she gets free," beamed Claude, full of confidence. "Otherwise, she'll fly about the room and chuck soot everywhere . . . so don't frighten her and don't criticise her . . . she takes criticism very personally, and gets into a flap, and in her state right now, that could cause a lot of mess."

Gingerly, he had removed the drape, but there was no sign of the hen. Alfred had sniffed and wagged his tail, looking at Claude for guidance, but Claude was puzzled.

"Clara?" he shouted up the chimney. But there was no response. "Don't say she's roosting on one of those ledges!" he had cried, shouting again, "Clara? Have you gone to sleep on the job? Down, down, you daft ha'p'orth . . ."

Alfred barked his encouragement, so Claude said, "I'll have to go up the ladder again to shout at her, Mrs Crowberry, Alfred will bark and then she'll come down . . ."

"I hope you don't let that bird make a mess . . ."

Claude had replaced the drapes just in case Clara made a dramatic return to the living room and went outside to repeat the performance, with Alfred barking from below. But as Claude reached the top of his ladder to peer down the chimney, Clara had fluttered out, dazzled by the light and smothered with soot. She had tried to settle on the rim of the chimney pot for a well-earned breather but her present state militated against her. With soot in her eyes, she could not see what she was doing and had missed her footing to flutter down the chimney — but it was the one which led into Abraham's study.

As she flapped and cackled her way down the second chimney, attempting in the darkness to find a foothold on one of the little ledges, so mountains of soot and black carbon debris preceded her. Unfortunately, there was no protective drape in that other room and as the hen's raucous cackling echoed down the chimney, so Alfred heard her calls and galloped through to the other room. He stood and barked up the chimney as cascades of soot came down to the sound of Clara cackling aloft. And when the soot fell, it had mushroomed into the room to smother the recumbent Abraham, his paintings, the floor and every surface, including the sparse furnishings. Within a very short space of time, the entire room had been filled with a cloud of thick black dust. Abraham had coughed and spluttered; Alfred had barked; the hen had cackled and Claude had shouted his distress from above as the hen, fluttering up and down the chimney and performing a first-class soot removal exercise, caused hundredweights of the stuff to fall into the room. She really was doing a first-class job.

Most of it landed on Alfred, barking his instructions from below. Amelia dashed in to see what was happening.

"You'll have to do something about this," coughed Abraham, his face blackened with two eyeholes peering out.

"No! You do something about it! I'm going to report that man for cruelty to a hen!" she had snapped.

"Me?" had responded the sooty Abraham. "Me do something?"

Leaving Clara stuck up the chimney, Alfred paddling through a mountain of soot, Claude doing his best to persuade Clara to rise from the top and Abraham wondering what to do about it all and whether he needed a brush and shovel, Amelia had come to see me.

"I want that man reported for cruelty to that hen!" she demanded with all the authority of her own rarefied breeding as she stalked out.

"I'm not sure the courts would accept it as cruelty." I tried to explain the difficulties of such a prosecution to her. "Clara is not a wild bird, so the Protection of Birds Act does not apply so we'd have to consider the Protection of Animals Act of 1911, and the offence of causing unnecessary suffering to Clara. Because she is a domestic fowl, she is included within the term 'animal' for cruelty purposes so the courts might accept a prosecution . . . it depends upon whether Claude was cruel, though, and . . ."

"Constable, you must not shirk from your duty!" She was now in full flow. "I shall expect to hear from you in due course, and I shall be a witness for the prosecution. Come to me for a statement when you are ready to proceed!"

Sergeant Blaketon was most uneasy about recommending a prosecution, thinking he would be laughed out of court, but the threats from someone of noble birth, a wildlife campaigner and conservationist to boot, persuaded him to submit the necessary report to the superintendent for consideration.

"Go and get a statement from that woman," he said to me several days later. "The one consolation is that I'll get Greengrass in court for something!"

But when I got to Rigg Side Cottage, I found Abraham lying on the settee with the soot solidifying all around him.

Nothing had been touched, nothing had been cleaned up and I got the impression my arrival had roused him from his slumbers.

"Where's Amelia?" I asked him.

"No idea, Constable," he said. "She's left me. She says she wants a divorce. And if you want to know where she is, I have no idea. She left no address. But you'd think she would have tidied the place up before she went, wouldn't you?"

"Will you be a witness against Greengrass, for cruelty to that chimney sweeping hen of his?" I put to him.

"No way, Constable, I don't like trouble," he said, and curled over and went back to sleep.

Without a witness, we could not hope to prosecute Claude Jeremiah Greengrass for cruelty to a hen, at which Sergeant Blaketon said, "Rhea, if that man ever cleans a chimney again with a hen, let me know! I will get a witness to say it's cruel . . . I will have that man in court, I will, so help me!"

"Yes, Sergeant," I said, wondering about the legal situation if Claude had dropped a pheasant down the chimney. They are not classed as wild birds nor are they domestic — and would a capercaillie or a ptarmigan do a better job?

* * *

On another occasion, I received a furious telephone call from Alec Mullen, a wholesale greengrocer in Ashfordly, during which he demanded that I arrest Claude Jeremiah Greengrass and charge him with committing false pretences. It arose from the following incident which Mr Mullen explained to me.

On a hot summer day, one of Claude's pigs escaped and made for a nearby patch of woodland where it began to unearth some plants. It worked at a furious rate, grunting and using its snout in what could be described as a frenzy. It was behaving like that when Claude, with Alfred the dog at his heels, located the animal. The moment Alfred arrived, however, he also began to dig nearby at a similarly manic pace with his front paws. Pig and dog seemed to be competing with one another for some prize, each concentrating on its own patch of earth as they dug into the light earth. Alfred was as keen as the pig to reach whatever was hidden below the ground. When Claude entered the fray by recovering one of the objects from Alfred's jaws, he shouted. "Truffles! They've found a truffle patch!"

The pig was eating them as fast as it could unearth them and Claude then realised that unless he drove the pig from its happy hunting ground, it would consume all the truffles. Finding a stout piece of fallen wood on the ground, Claude managed to drive the pig away, a comparatively difficult task.

Then, ordering Alfred to "Drop it" and to "Heel", he succeeded in returning the animals to his ranch, unhappy though they were about being dragged from such an appetising place.

A truffle is a type of fungus which grows under the ground close to the roots of trees, especially beech trees, and they are to be found in Britain as well as on the continent. It is virtually impossible for humans to locate truffles, therefore animals are used — some animals can smell them from as far away as 100 metres — and Claude knew that they were much sought after by gourmets, restaurant owners and hotel keepers.

High-quality truffles command high prices because they are valuable additives to top-quality food and even though they do not taste very nice in themselves, they do add an exquisite flavour to the food with which they are cooked. In France, truffles are used to make *pâté de foie gras*.

Both pigs and dogs are used to locate them. Dogs, especially Spanish poodles, are favoured as truffle-hunters because pigs tend to eat their finds before they can be retrieved by the human hunters. In Claude's case, both his pig and his dog were now known to be capable of locating these underground gems and Claude knew that there was money to be made from truffles. Claude reasoned that if he could prevent his pig from eating them the moment it located them, he could deploy both pig and Alfred in frequent truffle-hunting expeditions; working together, they could harvest hundreds of truffles and make a fortune. But who would buy them?

George at the pub could have only a modest demand for them, and then Claude realised that a wholesaler might provide the answer, bearing in mind that the harvesting and use of a truffle had both to be completed within three or four days. If they are left unused for longer than that, they tend to lose some of their flavour; when underground, truffles appear and ripen within a couple of days or so. The discovery of truffles is indeed a very fine art which requires rapid action.

There was no time to lose. From the village kiosk, Claude rang Mullens Greengrocers in Ashfordly to ask if they were interested in buying truffles.

"Truffles?" cried Alec Mullen. "I didn't know we had truffles hereabouts?"

"Aye, well, it's a secret patch, you see, it's just been discovered," Claude explained. "My pig found 'em this morning, and my dog. My Alfred's a highly trained truffle hound and we could fetch a supply this afternoon — for a price that is."

"I've never dealt in truffles before, there's not been much call for them hereabouts. Folks seldom eat truffles with roast beef and Yorkshire pudding."

"They're for gourmets, Mr Mullen. Specialist chefs use 'em, the French use 'em . . ."

"Although I've never dealt in truffles, I've heard all about them, Mr Greengrass. Look, you fetch me a supply and in the meantime, I'll have a ring around some of the retailers I deal with to see if we can get 'em interested. How much will you be charging?"

"Aye, well, that's summat we'll have to discuss, you see. I mean, there's my labour and transport, and they are a bit special; Queen Victoria loved 'em, you understand. You might be talking of two pounds a pound at least . . ."

"That's not a bad price for good truffles," said Mr Mullen. "Right, fetch 'em in and not a word to other greengrocers, right? I want the monopoly on these and I'll pay extra for the privilege!"

"My word is my bond," oozed Claude, replacing the receiver. Outside the kiosk, he turned to Alfred and beamed. "Come on, Alfred, we've work to do. I'm not employing that pig, she'll eat the lot . . ."

During the course of my duty that evening, I called in the pub and was rather surprised to find Claude buying celebratory drinks for the regulars. It wasn't often he spent money on other drinkers.

"So what's the occasion, Claude?" I asked.

"I'm in the big time now, Mr Rhea, a touch of class, a new line in business. I'm finding my true vocation now, gourmet foods and all that. Greengrass Gourmet Foods, that's me."

"I don't believe it! Does that mean you're selling pheasants legitimately?"

"It's nowt to do with pheasants, Constable. It's truffles. I've discovered that my Alfred is a top-quality truffle hound and we've located a truffle patch; it's in a secret location, of course."

"Truffles? In Aidensfield? I thought they only grew in France?"

"Aye, well, that's where you're wrong. They used to grow in Wiltshire, see, and now they've been found in Aidensfield. My pig found a patch this morning, and Alfred is now chief sniffer."

"Alfred, a truffle hound?"

"The best for miles around, Mr Rhea. By, he does go at it, you'd think he was digging for gold . . . He's earning me a fortune. I might have to get his nose insured, you need a very delicate nose for finding truffles. Anyroad, I sold five pounds of 'em this afternoon, at two pounds a pound . . . that's money, Constable, good money."

At this news, I turned to George and asked, "Are you using Claude's truffles in your meals?"

"I'm not paying two pounds a pound for summat his dog has dug up!" snapped George. "Besides, my customers don't exactly go in for gourmet meals. They're happier with chicken and chips in a basket and allus want mint sauce with their mutton, not some wizened old root that Claude wants rid of."

It was the following morning that Alec Mullen rang me.

"PC Rhea, Aidensfield," I answered in the usual way.

"I have a complaint to make, Constable." He sounded very angry. "It's a case of fraud."

"Who are you complaining about?" I asked. "And what is the nature of your complaint?" I wondered why Mullen had not contacted Ashfordly Police Station.

"Claude Jeremiah Greengrass." He spoke the words with venom. "He's fiddled me, he's made me the laughing stock of my profession."

"What's he done now?" I asked.

"He sold me a box of what he said were truffles," Mr Mullen spoke slowly. "I mean, Constable, I'd never seen a truffle in my life, would you believe, but I took Claude at his word."

"So they're not truffles?"

"No they are not!"

"So what are they?"

"Pignuts," he spat out the word. "Pignuts, Constable, that grow wild in their millions around here."

"But his pig found them," I said.

"Pigs do," he cried. "And so do dogs. Pigs and dogs will dig for pignuts, Mr Rhea, so just you get yourself out to those woods with Greengrass and ask him to show you that truffle patch. I'll bet it's covered with a flower that looks like wild parsley or cow parsley, but underneath it there are pignuts. You dig under the roots with a knife and gently take them out . . . kids love them, Mr Rhea. In the past, country folk would dig them up and eat them, but they're not truffles. I've been conned, Constable, and I want action."

"I'll have words with him," I promised.

When I arrived at the Greengrass ranch, Claude was about to embark on another truffle-hunting mission. Alfred was at his side, tail wagging in anticipation, having been given a sniff of the basket that Claude was carrying. I decided not to reveal Mullen's claims just yet.

"How about showing me your truffle patch, Claude?"

He was clearly puzzled about my unexpected arrival. "Nay, Mr Rhea, it's confidential, a businessman can't reveal his secrets."

"Suppose they are not truffles?" I put to him. "Suppose you are selling them under false pretences?"

"If that's what you think, then mebbe you had better come and see for yourself, Constable!" he said.

At that stage, I could see that he believed they were genuine truffles. We trudged across his land towards the wood, and then he let Alfred off the lead. Alfred galloped ahead and was soon digging furiously beneath a tree.

"There you are, Constable," Claude beamed. "Another truffle . . . by, he's the best truffle hound for miles. Sit, Alfred, sit!"

Alfred, with evident reluctance, obeyed his master and sat as Claude produced a long knife and gently unearthed the root which had attracted Alfred, and he held it up for my inspection.

"There you are, Constable, a genuine truffle fresh from the ground."

"It's a pignut, Claude," I said gently. "That plant is a relation of the wild carrot, it produces a tasty root which you've just dug up. Pigs and dogs will dig for them . . ."

"But I thought this was a truffle . . ." There was genuine concern on his face now.

"Mr Mullen is not very happy about it," I interrupted him. "In fact, he's furious, he wants me to prosecute you for false pretences."

"False pretences? But he bought 'em off me, he thought they were truffles."

I took a specimen with me and decided the best method of approaching the problem, before launching into an official police prosecution, was to take the object to Mr Mullen for his inspection. I drove into Ashfordly and found him at his shop.

"Yes, that's what he's been selling me," he acknowledged. "My customers sent them all back to me this morning."

"But you thought they were truffles?" I put to him. "And you sold them to your customers as truffles. So you are as guilty as Claude."

"He told me they were truffles, Constable."

"He honestly thought they were, Mr Mullen, just as you did. I'm not protecting him, I'm just trying to imagine what a court of law might think if we went ahead. The publicity might destroy your reputation — it might suggest that Mullens don't know a pignut from a truffle . . ."

"I'd never seen a truffle, or a pignut for that matter, but I was angry," he said. "And embarrassed . . . my customers were most indignant, some were infuriated about it all."

"They'll get over it, I'm sure," I said. "Better if just your customers know about this, rather than the entire town and surrounding villages reading about it in the papers."

Alec Mullen decided not to proceed against Claude provided the old rogue compensated him for his outlay. I returned to Aidensfield and drove straight to Claude's house where I found him having his coffee break. He looked rather gloomy but offered me one and I accepted, sitting down at his table. It was laden with pignuts and other odds and ends. "Mullens are not going to prosecute, Claude."

His face showed his relief. "It was an honest mistake, but what am I going to do with all those pignuts?" He indicated his recently harvested pile on the table.

"Give them to the pigs?" I smiled. I picked up a handful to see if they had any scent but there, nestling among them, was a strange, knobbly object with a dark brown skin which was almost black, and it was about the size of a golf ball. This was not a pignut . . .

"Claude!" I said. "You've found a truffle."

He smiled and said he would give it to Alex Mullen, as a gift.

9. GREENGRASS TO THE DOGS

His faithful dog shall bear him company.
ALEXANDER POPE, 1688–1744

There can be no doubt that Alfred the lurcher was devoted to Claude Jeremiah Greengrass and it is equally true that Claude was devoted to his dog. The pair went almost everywhere together and each appeared to have an instinctive understanding of the moods and intentions of the other. This might have resulted from the fact that a good poacher needs a good dog, one which is cunning and to some degree independent while at the same time being obedient and loyal to its master. A poacher also needs a dog which understands the ways of both nature and man, especially if that aspect of nature is a pheasant, and the man in question is the lawful gamekeeper whose duty is to care for that pheasant,

Alfred was such a dog. Flea-ridden perhaps, not the most handsome of creatures either but steadfast towards his lord and master; he was Claude's best friend and, like his master, he had an instinctive distrust of landowners, gamekeepers, police officers and people who owned shooting rights.

With dozens of laws, rules and regulations governing the keeping of dogs, it was inevitable that the paths of Alfred and

I would cross from time to time. Sometimes he was with his master, sometimes he was alone, but whenever he was alone, I knew that Claude was not far away. Like lots of local dogs, Alfred had his calling places.

These were friendly households who would allow him to sit by their fireside or have a scrap to eat. Claude would often be in the same house at the same time, having a cup of tea or a chat — if the household welcomed Claude, it also welcomed Alfred and just as Claude liked to visit several widows in Aidensfield, so Alfred would lustily pursue the lady dogs of the village, particularly when they were in heat. This was not one of his most endearing habits, however, and often resulted in him receiving a wallop with a broom handle or a kick in a rather painful place.

Whatever Claude's many faults, he never knowingly allowed Alfred to wander out of control, and he knew the rules about dogs running loose at lambing time. In many ways, Alfred was a fine example of the way a countryman's dog should be loved and cared for. Nonetheless, whenever Alfred noticed my uniformed arrival, he would slink away to warn his master of my presence so that sometimes I would decide to check whether he was wearing a collar, whether his licence was up-to-date or whether his behaviour was likely to cause worry to livestock or lead to complaints that he was not kept under control. His only weakness was lady dogs on heat and he would occasionally defy Claude to embark on a journey of joy and romance. If Claude knew there was a bitch on heat anywhere within a five-mile radius, he would keep Alfred on a lead or ensure he was kept in an escape-proof place.

It was with some surprise, therefore, that one afternoon I received a light-hearted complaint about Alfred's behaviour. It seemed he had sneaked into the canteen of the village school and had run off with a string of raw sausages. Cook had shouted at him, but the wilful dog had fled to consume his trophy at leisure.

Later the same afternoon, the butcher rang me to say Alfred had snaffled a pork chop from the counter and then I was told he had entered a house near the pub to abscond with a leg of chicken — all within the space of a couple of hours.

Thinking this was highly unlike Alfred's general behaviour, the combined complaints nonetheless meant I had to pay a visit to Claude's establishment to get him to halt his dog's dishonest antics. Claude was feeding his hens as I drove down the rough, muddy track and I noticed Alfred was nearby, lying asleep in a patch of afternoon sunlight.

"I've been having complaints about your dog!" I said, after parking the van.

"Look, Constable, when a bitch is on heat, he's like me — uncontrollable."

"Complaints about him stealing, Claude, and shoplifting."

"My Alfred is no thief, Constable! He's like me, well brought up and honest."

I outlined the complaints and Claude shook his head. "Nay, lad, it's not him. He's been here with me all afternoon; we've been fencing and ditching. Never been away from the place, neither me nor him."

"A good alibi, eh?" I said. "Look, Claude, Alfred is a most distinctive dog, there's no other dog like him and I have at least three witnesses to say he was the raider."

"I'd say my Alfred was being set up for those crimes, Constable, it'll be some other dog, disguised to look like him. There might be a Fagin who's training dogs to go out and nick household goods, eh? Think of that . . ."

"Claude, this is serious. You know what happens to dogs that are not kept under proper control?"

"You'd never have Alfred put down when he's innocent, would you? This is victimisation of the innocent, Constable, and there could be a miscarriage of justice if you're not careful. Alfred is innocent, mark my words."

Knowing I would never persuade Claude to admit that Alfred had strayed that afternoon, I returned to Aidensfield village and informed the complainants of my action, saying Claude would ensure Alfred would behave in the future. But he didn't. In the days that followed, several householders told me they had chased Alfred out of their kitchens after he'd grabbed a mouthful of food, on one occasion vanishing with half a pound of butter between his teeth. Someone else had seen him chasing hens about a paddock, a farmer had ejected him from a milking parlour whereupon the fleeing dog had knocked over a pail of fresh milk, and a cat owner had heard a kerfuffle upstairs which, it had transpired, was Alfred cornering the cat on top of a wardrobe.

On each occasion, Claude had an alibi for Alfred. In one case, Claude had been motoring on the road between Ashfordly and Aidensfield at the time Alfred was accused of raping a miniature dachshund — and Alfred had been in the vehicle with Claude, having been to the vet for some treatment. I checked the times of the alleged misconduct with the time Alfred had been injected by the vet and it was impossible that Alfred could have been the culprit. But who would disguise their dog as Alfred?

The answer came a few days later from Claude himself. In a state of some excitement, he came hammering on my office door one lunchtime and said, "Constable, come to my place right away. I've summat to show you."

"What is it?" I was wary of anything Claude might wish me to do.

"The solution to the Aidensfield crime wave!" he grinned, and so I followed his old truck in my minivan. I noticed that Alfred was in the front passenger seat but when we arrived at the ranch, Claude led me to an outbuilding and there, incarcerated behind a stout wooden door, was an exact replica of Alfred.

"How about that, then?" beamed Claude. "It means my Alfred is innocent, like I said all along."

"I'm sorry I doubted your word, Claude, but who is this chap?" The likeness to Alfred was astonishing — even at close quarters the dogs were like twins, even down to the sly look in the eyes and the greyish white curly hair. I noticed the dog was wearing a collar but it contained no name and address.

"I reckon it's Alfred's twin brother, come to pay us a family visit," smiled Claude. "I found him in my kitchen, helping himself to Alfred's dinner."

"Alfred wouldn't be very pleased about that!" I quipped.

"He never batted an eyelid, Constable, he went over and sniffed at the visitor, then they shared the grub. Blood's thicker than water, eh?"

"Blood? You mean these dogs really are related?"

"I am serious, Constable. This really could be Alfred's twin brother, returning to his roots. There was two of 'em, you know, when Alfred was born. I reared 'em both; the other was bought by a chap in Strensford."

"Who was it? Can you remember? Maybe we could contact him?"

"I've no idea, Mr Rhea. He turned up here one day with a smart car full of kids and bought that pup for cash. A fiver he paid, if my memory serves me right. But you know what I think?"

"Tell me, Claude."

"I think the owner couldn't cope; lurchers are country dogs, Constable, and need wide open spaces. That chap was a townie. I reckon he's driven out to these moors and chucked that dog out of his car, abandoned him, left him to fend for himself. Folks do that, you know, when they grow tired of looking after dogs."

"I know they do, Claude, and it's heartless. So are you going to keep this stray?"

"Well, I may as well hang on to him for a day or two, in case anybody comes looking for him. I mean, I may be wrong about him being a stray. He could have run away, be somebody's pet and is hungry. There may be an advert in the paper at the weekend, eh?"

"It's possible. Right, I'll make a note in our records in case anyone reports him missing. Now, Claude, I really do appreciate your concern for that dog. You'll keep him locked up, though? We don't want folks complaining again, especially if they think it's Alfred. I'll tell those people who've complained to me that Alfred is innocent," I assured him. "So, it seems your family's expanding."

"If I feed him well enough, he won't go stealing grub from folks' homes." Claude sounded very positive.

Three weeks later, there was no indication in our records that anyone had reported the Alfred-look-alike as missing from home, nor had Claude received any communication from an anxious owner. It seemed Claude had acquired a second Alfred — and he called the new arrival Ambrose. One sunny afternoon, I noticed Claude walking down the street with both Alfred and Ambrose in tow, both clearly under training. I noticed that Ambrose was wearing one of Alfred's old collars, complete with Claude's name and address. To my mind, this indicated that Claude was taking his new responsibilities very seriously and he told me that Ambrose appeared to have ceased his travels now that he was being well fed and cared for. Certainly, the dog seemed very content with its new life.

"So you're keeping him, are you?" I put to Claude.

"May as well," he said, "I don't want to see him put down, and it seems nobody's worried about him."

"You'll need a dog licence for him," I said,

"Dog licence?" There was horror on Claude's face at my suggestion and he began to blink — then he shook his head. "No, Constable, I'm exempt."

"Exempt? Of course you're not exempt. You are the keeper of that dog; you don't have to be the owner to be responsible for getting a dog licence. If a dog's in your care or custody, or on your premises, the law says you are the keeper. And if you are the keeper, you must take out the licence."

"Aye, I know all about that, but packs of hounds are exempt, aren't they?"

"Packs of hounds? But Ambrose isn't a pack of hounds?"

"Him and Alfred are!" beamed Claude. "How many hounds does it take to make a pack? I'll bet that's summat old Blaketon hasn't thought about, eh? These two dogs are hounds, Constable, and I'm running a pack of 'em! You might even say I was the master of hounds, eh? Mebbe I should get a pink jacket?"

"I'll have to check on that!" I said, not being totally sure of the law governing packs of foxhounds and their liability for dog licences. Leaving Claude to think he had triumphed, I went home and took my *Moriarty's Police Law* off the shelf to check on the exemption for hounds. To give Claude his due, there was no definition of the term "hound", consequently it could apply equally to foxhounds, bloodhounds, otter hounds and, one might suppose, to any other sort of hound. I was not sure whether, for legal purposes, there was a distinction between a hound and a dog and didn't think Elvis Presley's song "Hound Dog" was any help. However, when I read further into the Act, I discovered that the exemption applied only to hounds under the age of twelve months which belonged to a master of hounds and which had never been entered in or used in a pack of hounds. Untrained hound pups in other words.

I returned to Claude, clutching my copy of *Moriarty*.

"Claude," I said, as he settled me at his table and I opened the book at the required page. "You may be a master of hounds, Alfred and Ambrose may well be the hounds in question, but the exemption from a licence applies only to hounds under twelve months of age which have not been entered in or used in a pack of hounds. I reckon yours are more than twelve months old. I know Alfred is more than twelve months old, and you said Ambrose was his twin brother." He blinked at me as I went on, "And they have been used in a pack. I saw you, Alfred and Ambrose walking down the street nicely under control and being trained, which they would be, with you being the master of hounds and they being the pack, small pack though it is! Claude, the short message is that you need a licence for Ambrose."

"How about if Alfred and Ambrose are sheep dogs?" he asked. "I mean, I do keep a flock on the moor."

"Dogs used *solely* for tending sheep or cattle on a farm, or in the exercise of the calling of a shepherd, may be exempt if their owners get a certificate of exemption to prove that's all the dogs do. You would have to make a declaration to that effect; you'd not have to use them for anything other than tending sheep or cattle, and then you'd have to go to court to make your claim for a certificate of exemption."

"Court?" He was horrified at the idea.

"Yes, the magistrates court, not one of your favourite places, I believe. Look, Claude, don't be so daft. You need a dog licence for Ambrose, it's as simple as that, so get yourself down to the post office for one and I'll be back in a week to inspect it!"

He blinked at me and said nothing as I left.

In the days that followed, there were no further complaints about Alfred-look-alikes raiding the homes and business premises of the people of Aidensfield and I believed that Claude was performing a very useful task in rehabilitating his visitor. When I saw him and Alfred heading towards the pub for their lunch one day, I took the opportunity to halt the pair and to ask about Ambrose's dog licence.

"No need, Mr Rhea," Claude said. "He's gone. Upped and left without so much as a word of thanks."

"Ambrose, you mean?"

"Aye. He had his breakfast yesterday, cleaned it all up and then just walked out. I spotted him trotting up the hill towards the main road . . . I shouted but he just kept going; I went after him in my truck, but he'd vanished. He's not come back and I don't think he ever will."

"A wanderer, eh?"

"It's the gypsy blood in him, Constable. I reckon he didn't want owt to do with licences and officialdom, you see . . ."

And he blinked at me as he stooped to stroke Alfred.

* * *

For all Claude's control over Alfred, the lusty male dog did break Claude's curfew once in a while, invariably when there was a bitch on heat somewhere in the locality. Alfred would scent the air, follow his nose and sometimes disappear for days leaving Claude worried and sleepless at the thought of Alfred coming to some harm or being locked up as a stray. But the inbred cunning of the animal ensured he was never caught and that he always returned home with a triumphant air about his lithe, muddy and tired body.

In reaching the object of his desire, Alfred proved, on occasions, to be something of genius. He would travel up to four or five miles in search of love and instead of walking, he would hitch a lift. Many is the time he was found hiding under one of the seats of Arnold Merryweather's bus, sitting on the rear platform of a dustcart or even lying among the crates of a brewer's lorry. In all cases, he seemed to know where he was heading and always reached his destination by the simple device of snapping and snarling at anyone who tried to remove him. In time, the locals who found Alfred inside or upon their vehicle allowed him to remain, knowing that he was upon a romantic mission of desperate urgency.

By and large, his roaming did not concern me, unless, of course, there was a suggestion that Alfred was attacking moorland sheep or being dangerous in any way. There could have been claims that Claude did not have the dog under proper control on such excursions, but to bring in the force of law on such an occasion would have been too heavy-handed. As long as Alfred went about his love-life in a gentlemanly manner, few people were likely to object.

It was a combination of these factors, aided no doubt by Alfred's realisation one sunny spring morning that there was a bitch on heat somewhere within sniffing distance, that did cause me a few problems. I was on routine patrol in my minivan when I received a radio call from Sergeant Blaketon; he was somewhere nearby in his official car and wanted a rendezvous because he had a task which required my presence — and his. I suggested meeting him at 11 a.m. in Aidensfield village street, near the War Memorial, and he agreed.

I had a few minutes in hand before the meeting and, having parked my van at the police house, patrolled the street on foot, chatting to the local people and popping into the pub for one of my routine visits. All was in order — the only customer was Claude Jeremiah Greengrass and he was discussing the flat season with George. Alfred was asleep before the fire. The relevance of that peaceful scenario was of material interest later that morning.

As the church clock was striking eleven, I strolled towards the War Memorial and, with split second timing, was followed by Sergeant Blaketon in his car. He pulled up, climbed out and savoured the fresh moorland air as the clock completed its eleven strikes. I noticed he left the driver's door open, something he would not normally do. He saw me looking at it.

"I dropped Ventress off before driving out here, Rhea," he explained. "Smoking like a chimney, he was. A draught of fresh air through the car will clear the smell, I hope. I might declare my car a no-smoking zone, Rhea. Open the other door will you? We can talk out here, in the fresh air."

We stood near the War Memorial as the breezes of Aidensfield began to purify the police car and, as we chatted, I noticed Alfred trotting along the street, albeit with no sign of Claude. I thought little of it at the time because Blaketon was explaining our task.

"I've had a report of vandalism, Rhea, at Ashfordly Cattery," Blaketon told me. "In fact, I've had several in recent weeks in other places where animals are confined. It could be the same culprit or culprits."

From what he told me, it seemed that someone was going around places where animals or birds were enclosed, and either cutting wire fences, knocking down barriers or opening gates to allow the animals to escape. Recent attacks included a battery hen unit, an aviary, a dogs' home, the zebra enclosure at a nearby zoo and now Ashfordly Cattery. There had not been any messages to claim responsibility, either by an organisation or an individual, but it did appear that someone felt that all creatures should have their freedom and not be caged or enclosed. So far, none of the escaped animals had been dangerous, although some were valuable, such as the birds released from the Elsinby aviary. What the culprits had failed to understand was that birds of that kind, and many of the animals, depended upon their captors for specialist food and accommodation. Most would undoubtedly perish in the wild, and that seemed to indicate the culprit or culprits were mentally unstable. There was always the possibility that, if such a person was mentally deranged, they would turn their attention to the big cats in the zoo or even cattle in a field. Sooner or later someone would get hurt.

"We've not made a public fuss about this, Rhea," Blaketon went on. "It's the sort of nutty behaviour that might tempt others of similar views to copy it, if we publicise it, and if the perpetrators have a grievance or a message for the world, it might encourage them to do more. We're adopting the softly-softly approach — observations, discreet enquiries and low-key investigations with the minimum of publicity. We don't want the nutters of Yorkshire turning all caged and enclosed animals loose."

Having outlined the problem, he suggested that I accompany him to the cattery at Ashfordly so that I could see the damage that had been done. He had brought Alf Ventress there earlier, and other rural constables would find themselves involved. If further acts of that kind were committed on my beat, on any of the poultry farms, dairy farms or even piggeries, then I may recognise the *modus operandi*. Entering his car, I was conscious of the prevailing smell and thought it was funny-smelling tobacco that Alf Ventress used, and so with the windows partly open we drove to the cattery, which was on the Aidensfield side of Ashfordly.

During the journey, Sergeant Blaketon told me that the cattery was owned and run by David and Eileen Easton, and that having established a thriving cat-breeding business, they had expanded into a cattery where people could leave their pets to either recuperate after an illness or lodge while their owners were away for any length of time. Many of the cats, some exotic in appearance, roamed free around the premises, but others, like those lodging there during their owners' absence, were kept in large, airy and clean enclosures surrounded and topped by sturdy, narrow-gauge wire fences. The cattery was known across a wide area and was regarded as a superb example where the animals received the best care and attention. The Eastons also wrote books and gave talks about all aspects of cat-keeping, ranging from its history to its hygiene.

The previous night, someone had cut the wire of several enclosures, thus allowing the cats to escape, and indeed several had. As they belonged to other people who had left them on trust, it was regarded as a very serious matter, hence the police involvement. Not all the cats had been caught and the cattery owners busily sought them immediately after contacting Ashfordly Police Station. A few had been located before Sergeant Blaketon's arrival with Alf Ventress.

Now it was my turn. Having briefed me fully on the case, Sergeant Blaketon drove off the main road and we entered a narrow lane at the head of which was a sign saying *Ashfordly Cattery. Proprietors: David and Eileen Easton. No dogs allowed*. After passing the sign, we drove down the long, winding lane into the isolated cattery and parked in the spacious yard in front of the house. As we climbed out of his car, he said, "Leave the doors open again, Rhea, we must get rid of that Ventress smell. I think he must smoke old socks or something. I've never known cigarette smoke to produce such a pong. The car will come to no harm here, we're well off the beaten track!"

We moved away to head for the front door, and by chance, I turned to look behind me — and saw Alfred sneaking out of Sergeant Blaketon's car! Now I knew what part of the pong had been! Dog! And not just any dog, a Greengrass dog!

"Sarge!" I said, calling him to a halt. "We've given Alfred a lift — I'll bet he's going courting!"

"Not that flea-ridden mutt of Greengrass's!" he snapped, turning around to look at the dog. But Alfred was loping away towards the drive, clearly heading for some pre-destined pleasure in Ashfordly. Then he saw a cat.

It was a beautiful blue Persian and it was halfway across the drive when Alfred spotted it; he barked and leapt towards it, all cats being fair game to a lurcher, and with an astonishing turn of speed, the cat galloped for safety. It headed for the place it knew best — the assemblage of cages — with Alfred in hot pursuit. He was barking furiously and within seconds, the faces of several other cats had appeared in the surrounding vegetation. Some stood their ground and spat, others rushed into the cattery and some shinned up trees. Quite suddenly, there were cats everywhere and Alfred had no idea which of them to chase. He barked at several in turn as others yowled and spat with all the ferocity of their species. There was pandemonium. At the sound of this commotion, David Easton ran from the enclosure armed with a yard brush, but he made the mistake of leaving the gate open. Alfred was inside like a shot, snapping at the heels of a cat which had dared to dart through in anticipation of safety. Suddenly, all the cats in the undamaged cases were clinging to the sides of their enclosures, spitting and yowling and crying with alarm as the woolly grey dog ran around, barking and snarling at every cat he could find.

Alfred had never had such a good time and he apparently forgot all about his amorous intentions because he raced around the cattery, barking and snarling at hundreds of cats in different positions and avoiding Sergeant Blaketon, me and David Easton, all of whom were now in pursuit.

"Sergeant Blaketon, you should not have brought your poodle here . . . it is a rule of this establishment . . ."

"That is not my dog!" Sergeant Blaketon came to a halt with all the majesty he could muster. "And it is not a poodle. No self-respecting poodle would look like that or behave like that. That animal belongs to a ne'er-do-well from Aidensfield, name of Greengrass, and if I were you, Mr Easton, I should sue him for damage and distress to your animals."

"But you brought him here, Sergeant, in your car!"

"He hitched a lift in my car without my knowledge," blushed Blaketon. "I had no idea he was with us, had I, Rhea?"

"No, Sergeant, and neither had I!" I confirmed. "He's done this before, hitched lifts from passing vehicles."

"Rhea, you will report Greengrass for failing to keep that dog under proper control and if he touches any one of those cats, I'll have him for worrying livestock, so help me!" snarled Blaketon.

"I don't think cats are regarded as livestock, Sergeant," I said, remembering a fiasco with a budgie that Alfred had worried. "Nor do I think a cattery will be regarded as agricultural land."

The offence of worrying livestock could only occur on agricultural land, and involved only cattle, sheep, goats, swine, horses, asses, mules and poultry. Not cats.

"Then find something to fit the circumstances," he snapped.

Our attempts to thwart Alfred in his rampage came to nothing; he dodged every attempt to corner him in the maze of cat enclosures, and succeeded in sending every cat to safety up trees or within their cages. Indeed, some had returned to the cages which had been vandalised, darting through the holes in the wire before clambering to the highest part of the netting. Some were spitting with anger and fright, others clung to their supports in abject fear but Alfred managed to keep well clear of our posse. Then he made a mistake. He rushed into a wire cage in pursuit of a ginger tom; the door was open and in a flash, Sergeant Blaketon slammed it shut.

Alfred was now a prisoner among hundreds of cats.

He began to howl pitifully the moment he realised his plight, sitting on his haunches and raising his muzzle as if to heaven to issue a most awful noise.

"Sorry about that," said Sergeant Blaketon, red-faced and highly embarrassed.

"So, what shall I do with that dog, Sergeant?" asked Easton, panting heavily as he placed the broom beside a wall.

"PC Rhea will contact his owner and get him to collect the dog. I suggest he remains here for a while, Mr Easton, to teach him a lesson, and I suggest you insist on some cash compensation before releasing that dog to its owner."

"Yes, I will do that. Now, I believe you came to inspect the damage caused by vandals, Sergeant?" Easton tried to appear very calm and in control as Alfred's mournful howling filled the air and disturbed the cats. "My wife would have shown you around, but she's gone to the dentist. So, where shall we begin?"

"A tour of the external enclosures, Mr Easton, I think. I thought Constable Rhea should see what they've done, so that he is aware of their MO."

I followed them around the premises and within ten minutes, the place had returned to a state of calm, except for Alfred's awful howling. It sounded as if he was facing death, and I believe the cats were distressed by the din, but there was nothing anyone could do. Alfred was destined to remain a hostage until a ransom was paid. I think his howling was due to frustrated love rather than concern over his current plight.

Having inspected the damage caused by the vandals, I recorded my impressions in my official notebook and we left, with Sergeant Blaketon still apologising for fetching Alfred on to the premises. He dropped me off in Aidensfield, with a reminder to tell Greengrass to collect Alfred as soon as possible, and ordered me to make very discreet enquiries about the vandalising of the animal enclosures. I found Claude at home; I told him what had happened and said he had been seeking Alfred around the village and was relieved when I said his dog was safe, but alarmed when I said it would cost him money to secure Alfred's release.

"How much, Mr Rhea?"

"How much are several hundred utterly terrified cats worth, Claude? He nearly caused havoc among those moggies..."

"I thought he'd gone courting," said Claude.

"I think you're right, Claude, but he hitched a lift with Blaketon. Not perhaps the most sensible of ideas in the circumstances."

"All right, I'll go and collect him, the daft old sod!" he sighed.

Two hours later, he was knocking on my office door and looked very upset when I confronted him.

"Have you seen my Alfred?" he asked quietly.

"Not since he was locked up," I answered. "Why?"

"Well, when that cattery chap's wife came home from shopping, she saw Alfred in the cage, howling his head off, and because he was upsetting the cats, she let him out. Her husband played hell with her, saying she should have asked first, but anyroad, it's too late. He's gone. He's off again, Mr Rhea."

"He'll be courting, Claude. I'll keep an eye open for him. He'll be safe, you'll see."

It was about midnight that same night when a domestic rabbit breeder on the far side of Ashfordly heard a noise outside. It was someone opening a metal gate which led into the premises. Inside the grounds were his hutches, all filled with show rabbits in excellent condition; his dog slept outside the house but had not raised the alarm on this occasion, but when the breeder, Alan Weaver, went out with his shotgun, he found a man about to loosen all the doors of the hutches. He was an animal rights campaigner called Simon Purdey and having locked the fellow in a secure outhouse, Weaver called Ashfordly Police.

He then went to see why his dog had not raised the alarm, thinking she had been doped by the intruder, but instead, found her *in flagrante delicto* with Alfred. Dog and bitch were locked together... Alfred was now incarcerated in a shed.

Alf Ventress drove out to fetch in the culprit — and he admitted the other crimes. He could not bear to see animals locked in cages — that was his only reason — but said he had not entered the premises via the front gate: he had come across the fields, in silence and in darkness.

"So who made the noise with the gate?" asked Ventress.

"It was that bloody dog of Greengrass's!" snapped Weaver. "I once saw him open my gate before, he puts his paw on the catch and bingo, he's in. He tried before to get at that bitch of mine and now he's got her. God knows what our Sally's pups will be like now that he's had his evil way."

"Well, he helped catch our man!" said Alf, who told me the tale next day.

Later I told Claude that Alfred was now securely locked in a shed among a lot of rabbits and he said, "Oh, not again! What's he done now?"

"You've got to go and collect him. He helped us catch a villain," I beamed. "He's a police informer, Claude."

Claude's face went a delicate shade of green.

"That dog allus lets me down these days . . . a copper's nark . . . I would never have thought it of a dog of mine. He's taken to mixing with some strange company these days . . . cats, rabbits and coppers! Whatever next?"

"He's going to be a dad," I said.

10. GREENGRASS AT CHRISTMAS

We'll keep our Christmas merry still.
            SIR WALTER SCOTT, 1771–1832

For the village constable of Aidensfield, the approach of Christmas meant three things: keeping an eye upon the nefarious activities of Claude Jeremiah Greengrass; cold and lonely turkey patrols, the name given to spot-checks on travelling vehicles in the search for stolen Christmas goodies; and rehearsals for the annual police entertainment in Ashfordly General Hospital. The officers of Ashfordly section always entertained the patients over Christmas and this included a lively party, the singing of carols, the appearance of Father Christmas and a distribution of presents which were provided from donations received from police and public alike during the preceding year.

Sergeant Blaketon regarded turkey patrols as the most important of these duties because one of his professional ambitions was to have Claude Jeremiah arrested for unlawful possession of Christmas fare. He knew Claude was prone to taking a few Christmas trees and sprigs of holly without permission and, inevitably, the old rogue was a prime suspect if turkeys were also stolen. I knew Blaketon would dearly like to have the fellow incarcerated in our cells on Christmas Day, if only to teach him a lesson. But to have Greengrass as a house guest in Ashfordly Police Station over Christmas did not appeal to me because it meant someone would have to be on duty to feed him — and probably to look after Alfred too. Maybe Blaketon would volunteer for those tasks? I doubted it.

It was well known among local policemen that even though other villains had been caught by Blaketon's network of cold country constables, Claude Jeremiah Greengrass always avoided capture. Somehow, though, he always had a plentiful supply of Christmas trees, holly and turkeys for his regular customers.

"So," Sergeant Blaketon said to me just before Christmas, "your next turkey patrol duty is at Gibbet Cross on Thursday night, 10 p.m. until 2 a.m. Stop all passing vehicles and search them for stolen property! And if you catch Greengrass red-handed, bang to rights in possession of stolen property, then I'll buy you a Christmas drink in the pub of your choice!"

Thus I was standing near the crossroads at Gibbet Cross one freezing December night during the week before Christmas. I'd walked from home because heavy snow was falling. The roads were becoming dangerous and it would be silly to risk taking a motor vehicle out in such conditions. It meant I had no shelter, though, and crashed my arms around myself to keep warm. I desperately wanted a vehicle — any vehicle — to come and give me something to do, but none did. The roads remained utterly deserted as they grew increasingly snowbound. Surely, I told myself, nobody would venture out on a night like this? My efforts were a waste of time but orders were orders. I could not abandon this duty without Blaketon's authority, so it seemed I would be here for four wasted hours.

Standing at that isolated spot, I shivered as the wind blew a flurry of snow into my face. As I played my torch across the landscape, it showed the snow was drifting. No cars would come now! If I'd had a radio, I would have called base to seek permission to conclude this duty, but I had no radio; I was out of contact. I was marooned in a growing blizzard on the North York Moors.

With snow rising around my ankles, I found myself thinking of the entertainment we were to provide at Ashfordly Hospital. At least it would be warm there! There would be mulled wine, hot mince pies with cream, and Christmas cake. It promised to be sheer bliss and I knew the patients eagerly awaited our concert. For years, the police officers of Ashfordly section had staged their concert in the day room, then toured the wards to entertain the patients, with Father Christmas visiting everyone who was bedridden. Every year, Sergeant Blaketon played the role of Father Christmas and dressed in red robes and a white beard. He made sure every patient, young or old, received a present. For the entertainment, some of us sang, some played musical instruments (Alf Ventress was particularly good on his trumpet), some told jokes and I did my conjuring act. As I stamped my feet to keep the circulation going, and waited lonely and cold at Gibbet Cross, I warmed to the thought of that forthcoming concert — it was on the Wednesday after Christmas so I must rehearse my Chinese linking rings, shrinking cards and disappearing billiard balls.

As I busied myself with my thoughts and mental rehearsals, I became aware of a vehicle heading cautiously towards me, its lights picking a slow passage through the thick snow. Who on earth had come out on a night like this? Peering through the whirling snowflakes, I flashed my torch at it.

The car skidded as its brakes were applied, but when it stopped I realised it was Sergeant Blaketon. He climbed out and said, "Pack it in, Rhea. Nobody in their right mind will go out tonight, let alone go thieving. Go home and put your feet up!"

"Thank you, Sergeant," I said. "I've not seen a single vehicle tonight — not till you came. I can't imagine anyone venturing out in this, we'll be snowed in by morning if this continues. Nobody in their right mind will drive in these conditions."

"Except silly old sergeants driving to give their constables instructions to go home, eh, Rhea?" he grinned.

Then, as if on cue, something was chugging towards us, heading gingerly down the hill towards our checkpoint with lights blazing. It sounded like a pickup truck and it was moving very carefully in the atrocious conditions. Blaketon smiled. It seemed we were in business.

"Hello, what's this, then? A customer? Somebody nicking turkeys and Christmas trees, thinking we'd all be sitting with our feet up, I'll bet!"

"One before we finish, Sarge!" I called to him. I meant my vigil had not been entirely in vain, even if the vehicle did contain an innocent person, so I waved my torch to halt it. I heard the brakes being applied — but it skidded in the soft snow. Suddenly, it seemed to be slithering rapidly towards Sergeant Blaketon . . . the thing was out of control on the hill as it turned sideways in the wet snow. The driver had lost control!

There was nothing anyone could do to halt the uncontrolled skid and Sergeant Blaketon tried to run from its path but he slipped in the snow then dived headlong into the ditch. He vanished headfirst into a deep snowdrift and I heard a muffled cry followed by silence as the oncoming vehicle slewed off the road so dangerously close to him. It just missed Blaketon's parked car and came to rest against a high, snow-covered verge with lights blazing and engine roaring.

I could see the rear of the truck was full of Christmas trees as the angry driver leapt out.

"What the . . ." It was Claude Jeremiah Greengrass and he was rather short of seasonal joy. "What a bloody stupid thing to do! You can't stop lorries in snow like this, especially going down hills . . . you daft bloody ha'p'orth! Oh, it's you, Constable . . . Well, I mean . . ."

"Blaketon's hurt." I ignored his outburst and flashed my torch into the drift as I ran towards the buried sergeant. "He's in there!"

All we could see was a pair of boots on the end of some dark trousers, so I began digging with bare hands to free him. Claude buckled down to help. The sergeant had gone head-first into the deep drift, like a diver from a high board, but he had encountered something rather more solid than newly fallen snowflakes. He'd hit his head on a stone or buried log. When we rescued him, he was unconscious with blood oozing from a head wound.

"I never did that!" Claude began. "I never hit him, did I?"

"No, he managed to get out of the way, Claude, by diving into that drift. But he's hit his head on something under the snow. Come on, he'll have to go to hospital in your pickup and be quick about it; there's room for us all and the weight of your truck will help us get through the snow. It's quicker than waiting for the ambulance."

"Aye, well, I mean, but . . ." I could see he was nervous about my proposal but went along with my suggestion.

We laid the unconscious Blaketon among the Christmas trees in the rear of Claude's old truck, covered him with Claude's old coat and some blankets from the police car, then set off. I remained in the rear to nurse Blaketon, the trees forming a cushioning effect as we trundled and slithered through the blizzard. I would collect the sergeant's car on our return trip and then take it home, snow permitting.

It was a mighty cold journey for me but we reached Ashfordly Hospital without any major mishaps and the duty doctor said Blaketon was concussed. He said he might soon regain consciousness, but he didn't. He lapsed into a coma which continued into the Christmas holiday. Instead of being available for duty, or to entertain the patients, he had become one. I must admit we were all very worried about him. None of us had ever seen our sergeant so vulnerable and helpless.

"Blaketon still hasn't regained consciousness, Nick," said Alf Ventress one day. "He's in a coma. We've tried all sorts to revive him, talking, making familiar noises, but nothing works. Nobody knows what'll bring him out of it. Poor old Oscar. So who's going to be Father Christmas for the hospital concert?"

As we pondered a suitable candidate, I remembered those trees in the back of Claude's pickup; I was sure they had not been lawfully obtained, but in the drama of that night, I hadn't had the time to check. Events had overtaken me and, as they'd be gone now, there was no way I could investigate the source of those trees without the necessary supporting evidence. Nonetheless, I reckoned Claude owed me a favour or two for past help I'd given him; I would ask him to play Father Christmas.

"You're not serious," he blustered when I went to see him. "*Me* play Father Christmas at a coppers' party?"

"I'm deadly serious, Claude, otherwise I might start asking about those trees you had in your truck that night." I tried a bit of bluff.

"Aye, well, I suppose I might just do it, not for your lot, mind, for the hospital and the patients, you understand." He blinked at me nervously.

And so, with Claude as Father Christmas, the entertainment went ahead. In the wards, our efforts were appreciated and then it was time for Father Christmas to tour the hospital. We had given the bearded, red-cloaked Claude a sack of parcels bearing the names of all the patients, young and old alike. He visited each bed in turn, chatting to the patients and making them laugh. He was surprisingly good in this role and his banter did cheer them up. And then he came to the final bed — Sergeant Blaketon's. For him, we had a rare edition of *Jane Eyre*, one of his favourite novels, but he was still unconscious.

Claude took the gift from his sack.

He spoke softly to me as he placed the parcel on the bedside cabinet. "I never thought I'd see Blaketon like this . . . it'll be a happy Christmas without him pestering me all the time! It's a right tonic for me, is this, seeing Blaketon out of commission." And suddenly, Claude leaned over the still form of the sergeant, grinned wickedly and shouted loudly into Blaketon's ear, "A happy Christmas, Sergeant Blaketon!"

"Greengrass?" With that, Sergeant Blaketon opened his eyes and jerked upright in bed. The first thing he saw was

Claude Jeremiah Greengrass and the vision caused his eyes to open wide in disbelief. Then he fell back as he shouted, "And where did you get those Christmas trees from? Lord Ashfordly's estate, was it?"

"I'm off," cried Claude.

He scuttled from the ward, ripping off his white beard as Blaketon's voice followed him along the corridors.

"Just you wait Greengrass! Running me off the road like that . . . and what about those Christmas trees? Where did you get them from? I haven't finished with you yet, Greengrass, so it's no good lurking inside those robes. I'll have you, Greengrass, so help me . . ."

Claude's familiar voice had done the trick; it had jerked Blaketon out of his coma and he was rapidly returning to his former self.

"I've just had a nightmare, Rhea!" he snapped, when he noticed my presence at his bedside. "I dreamt I saw Greengrass dressed up as Father Christmas. Anyway, what am I doing here?"

"Happy Christmas, Sergeant." We all gathered around his bed and began to sing, "While Shepherds Watched Their Flocks by Night".

* * *

In addition to the annual police concert at Ashfordly Hospital, there were many traditions in Aidensfield and one of them decreed that no one need be alone for their Christmas dinner. Every solitary person in Aidensfield was guaranteed companionship on Christmas Day if they wished. I was reminded of this when the widowed Mrs Brewster declined the villagers' invitation to the annual party.

While some people were invited in by friends and neighbours, others joined a community party at the village inn. A collection throughout the village during the year paid for the meal and any spare cash was used to buy logs for pensioners. As the village constable, I was a member of the committee which made these arrangements.

"So how many are coming, George?" I was making one of my regular calls at the pub.

"Fifteen so far." George had a list before him. "Including Sergeant Blaketon and Claude Jeremiah Greengrass — Claude never misses!"

"How about Mrs Brewster?" I asked. "Has she changed her mind?"

"She never comes," explained George. "She's waiting for that son of hers to return home. She puts logs on the fire, his slippers under his rocking chair, sets a place for Leonard, does turkey for two, pudding for two, even Christmas crackers for two."

"Where is he?" I did not know Leonard Brewster.

"He's dead, Nick. He caught the phantom coach, they reckon," explained George. "He left the house one Christmas Eve. It was blizzard conditions on the moors and all the roads into Aidensfield were blocked. He got lost in the snow somewhere on the old road to Lairsbeck. It's not used now, that road, it's overgrown with heather. But they never found him, Nick. There was no shelter up there; he must have died. He'd never have stood a chance of survival in that weather. It was all of twenty years ago. He'd be in his fifties now, if he'd lived."

"Why did he go up to the moor if the weather was so bad?" This puzzled me.

"He was in the Home Guard, Nick, it was wartime, 1944. He wasn't a regular soldier because he worked on a farm, but they reckon he saw a light on the moors, Christmas Eve it was. He wondered if somebody was in trouble out there, thought they needed help, so he went out to look. But he never came back. He vanished, Nick. Totally. Not a trace was ever found."

"There was a search for him?"

"Oh, aye, but not till next day when the alarm was raised. Everybody turned out. They had to cope with deep, drifted snow, but no one found anything. Not a sign, his body was never found, not even a bit of his clothing. Some said he'd caught the phantom coach, they reckoned it was t'only way anybody could have got off them moors in such a blizzard . . ." George laughed uneasily. "I mean, in that sort of snow, folks can lie buried for months. There's drifts twelve feet deep, with snow lasting till May or June . . . terrible conditions can develop up on those moors, and it happens so quickly."

"So his mother still waits for him on Christmas Day?"

George nodded. "Aye, just like the day he vanished. She'd got his dinner ready and waited for him to come home, but he never did. Even now, after all this time, she can't accept he's dead. If only they'd found something, a bit of his clothing, his boots, his watch . . . anything to let her know his fate, one way or the other. Nobody's ever found a sign of him from that day to this. She's been waiting ever since, poor old thing. His slippers are always under the rocking chair, waiting for Leonard."

"I'll have another word with her," I assured George. "I might persuade her to join the rest of the village for her Christmas dinner."

"Well, others have tried without persuading her, but she's welcome, Nick," smiled George. "Tell her that."

"I will," I promised. "Now, what's this about a phantom coach?"

"There was a terrible blizzard one Christmas Eve, blinding anybody who was daft enough to go out in it. The York-Pickering-Whitby stagecoach was routed through Aidensfield but that night, it took a wrong turning. You couldn't see a thing in that driving snow. The coach was empty, except for the driver and it was due to terminate at Whitby for Christmas. The driver couldn't see the road ahead and by mistake, he turned along the old road which goes over Jack Cross Rigg. The horses must have got terrified and bolted, and on the way into Lairsbeck, the coach ran away down a gradient, and the whole lot toppled over a precipice into the beck. The coachman was killed. Leonard Atkinson, he was. He's buried in our churchyard. They found him along with the wrecked coach and all four dead horses three days later. Nowadays, they say the phantom coach and four races along that old road on Christmas Eve with the coachman shouting and its lanterns showing through the blizzard . . . daft really, but you know how folks love yarns like that."

"So when Leonard Brewster vanished, they said he'd caught the phantom coach?"

"Aye, the weather was the same when he vanished, you see, Nick. It was Christmas Eve, and he *did* disappear without trace. Hereabouts, when anybody disappears on the moors, folks say they've caught the phantom coach. It's often seen before anyone vanishes . . . and folks do vanish up there."

"Our files contain lots of cases of people who have vanished on those moors." I knew that bodies could lie there for months without discovery. "But do people claim to have seen this phantom coach?"

"Oh, aye," George spoke seriously. "I remember one chap, driving a car he was, coming over them moors one Christmas Eve in a blizzard and he reckons he saw the lanterns of the coach. As he watched, the whole thing appeared through the snowflakes with horses galloping like fury. He thought it was a Christmas stunt by somebody. He saw it as clear as could be, the Neptune it was. He didn't stop or try to follow it because the weather was closing in, he had to get down off the moors before he got marooned."

"And others? Others have seen it?"

"Aye, Nick, over the years lots of folks reckon they've seen lights on a coach and four speeding over the moor from Adder Howe."

"Well, let's hope there's no blizzard this year and that nobody goes chasing lights!" I had no wish to be called out for a moorland search in such appalling conditions.

"It's not a good forecast, Nick, strong winds are likely and they say it'll be a white Christmas. There'll be blizzards on those tops."

"Then I hope everybody stays at home!" I smiled. "Well, I'll be off, George. I'll let you know if Mrs Brewster decides to come to your Christmas dinner."

When I went to see Mrs Brewster, she shook her head firmly.

"No thank you, Constable." She was firm in her resolve. "I do appreciate your kindness, but I shall prepare for Leonard. It would be dreadful if he returned and I was out. Suppose I hadn't a meal on the table when he comes home? That would be awful!"

She offered me a cup of tea and a scone as she explained how Leonard had seen lights on the moor that fateful night. Leaving his slippers under the rocking chair, he'd dressed in his storm-proof clothes then set off to investigate, carrying a powerful torch and using his ancestors' long crook-like stick to feel his way through the drifts.

She showed me a faded brown daguerreotype of her great-great-grandfather; he was standing beside a stagecoach and had the same long stick in his right hand, easily recognisable by the eagle's head which had been carved from a sheep's horn to form the handle.

"That's my great-great-grandfather, he was a coachman," said Mrs Brewster with pride. "He drove the Neptune on its route over the moors to Whitby."

The hairs on the nape of my neck stiffened. "Neptune?" he asked. "Isn't that the one which crashed in a blizzard?"

"Yes," she spoke softly. "He was the driver, my great-great-grandfather — Leonard Atkinson. The horses bolted in the blizzard and ran blind across the moor, Constable, along the wrong road. He couldn't halt them and they crashed over a ravine in Lairsbeck. It was in 1844, long before I was born. The family history keeps the story alive."

"So it was exactly a hundred years before your Leonard went out to investigate some lights on the moor?" I commented.

"Yes." Her voice softened. "It was a strange coincidence, wasn't it? Another odd thing was that my Leonard was carrying that very same eagle-headed stick when he was lost. It makes you think, eh?"

I tried to dismiss her statement as nothing more than coincidence aided by a strong imagination as I attempted once more to persuade her to join the others at the village inn. But she was steadfast in her refusal. She would wait for Leonard. I remember thinking it would be a long wait.

That Christmas Eve, I was on duty. At eleven o'clock in the evening, as the first flakes of snow were falling, I popped into the bars and lounge of the pub to wish George and his customers a Happy Christmas but George caught my arm and whispered, "You haven't seen Claude Jeremiah Greengrass, have you, Nick?"

"Not since lunchtime, no," I told him. "Why?"

"He's vanished. He said he'd seen a light on the moor then rushed off to investigate. That was two hours ago or more. I warned him that blizzards are forecast and . . ."

"Claude knows better than to stay out on a night like this!" I answered.

"Exactly, and he never misses a Christmas Eve in here."

"I'll check his ranch on my way home," I assured George, hoping Claude hadn't gone to catch the phantom coach. By the time I reached the Greengrass abode, walking instead of risking the minivan, the snow was falling in thick white clouds, obliterating everything and drifting as the wind began to strengthen. It was dry snow and it was lying. With astonishing speed, it began to fill recesses in the road, concealing the grass verges, making the moorland smooth and settling on my greatcoat until I looked like a walking snowman.

The wind was driving it across the great barren wastes of the higher moors and I knew what it must be like on those heights. My worries were increased when I saw there were no lights at Claude's house and I got no response as I hammered on the door. I tried the handle, but it was locked. The place was deserted.

"Claude?" I shouted. "Claude, are you there?"

Nothing. I searched the outbuildings as the dense falling snow muffled my shouts and I was turning to leave when I heard the familiar voice answering my call.

Claude was shouting, "Who's that?" as his snow-encrusted figure with Alfred his dog at his side, materialised through the blizzard. Alfred's woolly grey fur was matted with frozen snow. They looked a sorry pair.

"Claude?" I shouted. "Where have you been? We've been worried sick about you."

"I've seen a ghost, that's what. I need a drink, summat strong and hot! The phantom coach, up there." And he pointed in the direction of Adder Howe, shivering as he did so. "I saw lights, I thought somebody was lost, so me and Alfred went to search. He found summat, he was snuffling around under them big boulders. Anyroad, not long after I got there, I saw this coach and four hurtling across the moor with its lanterns burning then it vanished. It's right, Constable, as true as I'm standing here. Alfred ran off howling with me after him as fast as I could go — it's a good job he knew his way home or I'd have been a corpse out there. I'd have caught the phantom coach, believe me! I've never seen owt like them drifts, like mountains they are. Anyroad, he found this."

Claude opened his gloved fist to reveal an eagle's head carved from the horn of a sheep and containing the merest remnant of a rotted wooden walking stick. Even though it was severely weathered, I experienced a shiver down my spine. It was the handle of a crook-like stick.

"I think this belonged to Mrs Brewster's Leonard," I told him quietly.

The old rogue was silent as the flakes whirled about our heads, and then he said, "Aye, that's what I thought. He was a mate of mine, was Len, when we were younger. She'd best have this back, hadn't she? His mother, I mean."

"Yes," I said. "Are you going into the village, you could take it to her?"

"I was thinking I might just be in time for a stiff drink at the pub," said Claude. "Me and Alfred need warming up an' my fire's out, but by the time I get there, they'll be shut, I shouldn't wonder."

"Claude, if George closes on time at Christmas Eve, it'll be a miracle!" I said. "I won't be there to check, will I? And I do think you should be the one to give that eagle head back to Mrs Brewster."

"My Alfred found it among some rocks . . . There was nowt else, I had a look . . . animals and weather, you know, there's nowt left after all this time." There was sympathy in his voice. "Poor old Leonard. He caught the phantom coach right enough."

"Go and get a stiff drink, Claude, but see Mrs Brewster first!" I told him.

"Aye, right, I will."

I went home as he padded towards the village. Next morning, the snow lay thick and even, giving Aidensfield a picturesque Christmas appearance. Cottage lights glowed and fires flickered in cosy rooms as the people remained indoors.

Dinners were being prepared as the children opened their presents around the Christmas trees; lonely people were emerging to accept invitations; some were heading for the pub while others visited friends and neighbours. I decided to take a walk around the village and check a few houses before settling down to my own Christmas dinner with the family, chiefly to ensure that no one was deserted or too shy to take up their invitations. As I was walking past Mrs Brewster's window, I saw the rocking chair beside the fire.

The table was set for two and a Christmas tree with lights was glittering in a corner as the warm glow from the fire cast shadows about the cosy room of her cottage. I knocked and she answered.

"I came to see if you'd changed your mind about joining the others in the pub for your Christmas dinner," I said. "There'll be a good crowd there, you'd enjoy it and you'd be among friends."

"No, Constable, it's kind of you to remember me, but Leonard is home now," and she pointed into the room. I peeped around the door. In front of the fire, on a rug before the rocking chair, I saw a pair of man's slippers — and lying on the hearth was the eagle head Claude had found, the remains of the family heirloom. "He's asleep, he had a hard night, you see, out on the moors, but Claude found him and now he's back home. I mustn't wake him and I can't leave him now, can I?"

"No, of course not," I said, glancing at the chair. Then, not wishing to shatter her illusion, I said, "A happy Christmas to you both."

I left the cottage and as I walked back along the street, I glanced once more through her window.

Leonard's empty chair was rocking with the gentle motion of someone at peace.

THE END

ALSO BY NICHOLAS RHEA

CONSTABLE NICK MYSTERIES
Book 1: CONSTABLE ON THE HILL
Book 2: CONSTABLE ON THE PROWL
Book 3: CONSTABLE AROUND THE VILLAGE
Book 4: CONSTABLE ACROSS THE MOORS
Book 5: CONSTABLE IN THE DALE
Book 6: CONSTABLE BY THE SEA
Book 7: CONSTABLE ALONG THE LANE
Book 8: CONSTABLE THROUGH THE MEADOW
Book 9: CONSTABLE IN DISGUISE
Book 10: CONSTABLE AMONG THE HEATHER
Book 11: CONSTABLE BY THE STREAM
Book 12: CONSTABLE AROUND THE GREEN
Book 13: CONSTABLE BENEATH THE TREES
Book 14: CONSTABLE IN CONTROL
Book 15: CONSTABLE IN THE SHRUBBERY
Book 16: CONSTABLE VERSUS GREENGRASS
Book 17: CONSTABLE ABOUT THE PARISH
Book 18: CONSTABLE AT THE GATE
Book 19: CONSTABLE AT THE DAM
Book 20: CONSTABLE OVER THE STILE
Book 21: CONSTABLE UNDER THE GOOSEBERRY BUSH
Book 22: CONSTABLE IN THE FARMYARD
Book 23: CONSTABLE AROUND THE HOUSES
Book 24: CONSTABLE ALONG THE HIGHWAY
Book 25: CONSTABLE OVER THE BRIDGE
Book 26: CONSTABLE GOES TO MARKET
Book 27: CONSTABLE ALONG THE RIVERBANK
Book 28: CONSTABLE IN THE WILDERNESS
Book 29: CONSTABLE AROUND THE PARK
Book 30: CONSTABLE ALONG THE TRAIL
Book 31: CONSTABLE IN THE COUNTRY
Book 32: CONSTABLE ON THE COAST
Book 33: CONSTABLE ON VIEW

Book 34: CONSTABLE BEATS THE BOUNDS
Book 35: CONSTABLE AT THE FAIR
Book 36: CONSTABLE OVER THE HILL
Book 37: CONSTABLE ON TRIAL

MORE COMING SOON

Gorgeous new Kindle editions of the **Constable Nick** books soon to be released by Joffe Books.

Don't miss a book in the series — join our mailing list:

www.joffebooks.com/contact

FREE KINDLE BOOKS

DO YOU LOVE FREE AND BARGAIN BOOKS?

Do you love mysteries, historical fiction and romance? Join thousands of readers enjoying great books through our mailing list. You'll get new releases and great deals every week from one of the UK's leading independent publishers.

Join today, and you'll get your first bargain book this month!

www.joffebooks.com/contact

Follow us on Facebook, Twitter and Instagram

@joffebooks

Thank you for reading this book.

If you enjoyed it please leave feedback on Amazon or Goodreads, and if there is anything we missed or you have a question about, then please get in touch. The author and publishing team appreciate your feedback and time reading this book.

We're very grateful to eagle-eyed readers who take the time to contact us. Please send any errors you find to corrections@joffebooks.com. We'll get them fixed ASAP.

Made in the USA
Columbia, SC
19 May 2022